The second of eight children in a family often plagued by debt, **Charles Dickens** (1812–70) at ten saw his father arrested and confined in the Marshalsea, a debtors' prison in London, and although a small boy, he was placed in a blacking factory, where he worked at labeling bottles, visiting John Dickens on Sundays. Charles returned to school on his father's release, taught himself shorthand, and at sixteen became a parliamentary reporter. When he was twenty-four, his career took off with the publication of *Sketches by Boz* (1836), which was followed by *The Pickwick Papers* the next year. As a novelist and magazine editor, he had a long run of serialized successes through *Our Mutual Friend* (1865). His family life had ended earlier, in 1858, when fame drew him apart from his wife of twenty-three years, Catherine, and (although his readers never knew) into the arms of young Ellen Ternan, an actress. Ill health slowed him down but he continued his popular dramatic readings from his fiction to an adoring public that included Queen Victoria. At his death, he left *The Mystery of Edwin Drood* unfinished.

Regina Barreca, Professor of English and Feminist Theory at the University of Connecticut, is the editor of the influential journal *LIT: Literature, Interpretation, Theory*. Among her many books are *They Used to Call Me Snow White . . . But I Drifted*, a widely acclaimed study of women's humor, and *Babes in Boyland, It's Not That I'm Bitter . . .*, and *Untamed and Unabashed: Essays on Women and Humor in British Literature*. She is also the editor of *The Penguin Book of Women's Humor*.

Gerald Charles Dickens, British actor and great-great-grandson of Charles Dickens, brings to life his ancestor's works in his one-man performances. His *Christmas Carol* show, in which he portrays twenty-six characters, brought praise from the *New York Times*: "a once-in-a-lifetime brush with literary history." The *Boston Globe* called his performance "a Dickens of a show!" He also wrote, produced, and performs a biography of Charles Dickens entitled *Mr. Dickens Is Coming!*

CHARLES DICKENS

A
Christmas Carol
and Other Christmas Stories

With a New Introduction by

REGINA BARRECA

and an Afterword by

GERALD CHARLES DICKENS

SIGNET CLASSICS

SIGNET CLASSICS
Published by New American Library, a division of
Penguin Group (USA) Inc., 375 Hudson Street,
New York, New York 10014, USA
Penguin Group (Canada), 90 Eglinton Avenue East, Suite 700, Toronto,
Ontario M4P 2Y3, Canada (a division of Pearson Penguin Canada Inc.)
Penguin Books Ltd., 80 Strand, London WC2R 0RL, England
Penguin Ireland, 25 St. Stephen's Green, Dublin 2,
Ireland (a division of Penguin Books Ltd.)
Penguin Group (Australia), 250 Camberwell Road, Camberwell, Victoria 3124,
Australia (a division of Pearson Australia Group Pty. Ltd.)
Penguin Books India Pvt. Ltd., 11 Community Centre, Panchsheel Park,
New Delhi - 110 017, India
Penguin Group (NZ), 67 Apollo Drive, Rosedale, Auckland 0632,
New Zealand (a division of Pearson New Zealand Ltd.)
Penguin Books (South Africa) (Pty.) Ltd., 24 Sturdee Avenue,
Rosebank, Johannesburg 2196, South Africa

Penguin Books Ltd., Registered Offices:
80 Strand, London WC2R 0RL, England

Published by Signet Classics, an imprint of New American Library,
a division of Penguin Group (USA) Inc.

First Signet Classics Printing, November 1984
First Signet Classics Printing (Barreca Afterword), December 2011
10 9 8 7 6 5 4 3 2 1

Introduction copyright © Regina Barreca, 2011
Afterword copyright © Gerald Charles Dickens, 2008
All rights reserved

Contents

✦

Introduction

Many readers feel they know Ebenezer Scrooge before they encounter him on the page. They believe they'd recognize his pinched, wrinkled, and pointy features if they passed him on the street. That's because Scrooge has become an iconic figure. Like Captain Ahab, or Dr. Frankenstein, or Hester Prynne, Ebenezer Scrooge's character transcends and escapes the confines of the volume where he initially appeared. He wouldn't even need a scarlet letter; all he needs is a nightcap, a nightgown, and a sour, skeptical expression.

Iconic characters enter, wraithlike, into the wider, nonliterary culture as the embodiment of a particular set of qualities: if Ahab is obsession, Dr. Frankenstein, ambition, Hester, defiant virtue, then Scrooge, of course, is "engross[ed]" by his "master passion, Gain" (page 43).

The word "Scrooge" has even departed the character entirely, like a ghost leaving a body, and "Scrooge" now appears in dictionaries and in thesauruses as a synonym for "miser," "misanthrope," and "tightwad" with no mention of his Victorian textual origin.

Just as those who once cared for Scrooge watch his "nobler aspirations fall off one by one" until there is nothing left of him but his eager and then overwhelming avarice (page 43), so can those who are familiar with Dickens's original character watch him become caricatured into a two-dimensional version of his multidimensional sense.

And yet the essential Scrooge remains. There are award-winning musicals in which Scrooge is the star; there are child-friendly and Americanized Mickey Mouse versions of Dickens's novel where profit-sharing replaces philanthropy, and there are hundreds of stage and film adaptations of the Dickens work cherished by those who have never held the short book in their hands.

Like callow Scrooge at the beginning of the book, however, the unseasoned audience members of these productions don't know just how much they're missing until they've actually read the most significant Christmas book written in English.

Published in 1843, *A Christmas Carol* appeared the same year as the first commercially produced Christmas card. The card, of which 2,050 were printed, was commissioned by Sir Henry Cole and illustrated by John Callcott Horsley. It shows, triptychlike, a large, colorful central image of a prosperous family drinking wine (even a young child is drinking), which is bracketed by two smaller gray images portraying the poor and sick being given aid and succor. Although there are similarities in the outlines of the card and *The*

Christmas Carol, Dickens's novel is more than a mere holiday trifle to be discarded when the season has passed.

Word by carefully chosen word, Dickens engages the most troubling questions posed by philosophers, scholars, and theologians for millennia. He takes, for example, Genesis 4:9 ("Am I my brother's keeper?") and reframes it in an exchange between Scrooge and some philanthropically minded gentlemen who are attempting to "raise a fund to buy the poor some meat and drink, and means of warmth." The well-meaning fund-raisers explain, "We choose this time, because it is a time, of all others, when Want is keenly felt, and Abundance rejoices." Their argument is familiar enough. What is unexpected is Scrooge's famous reply: "I can't afford to make idle people merry."

Scrooge argues that, since he pays his taxes, he does his bit (an argument, we should note, still being made by various political caucuses today). "I help to support the [prisons and workhouses]—they cost enough," grumbles Scrooge. "[T]hose who are badly off must go there." When the gentlemen explain that many can't go there and that many others would rather die, Scrooge shrugs off their response with a simple "If they would rather die . . . they had better do it, and decrease the surplus population. . . . It's enough for a man to understand his own business, and not to interfere with other people's. Mine occupies me constantly. Good afternoon, gentlemen!" (pages 10–11).

During the course of one night, Christmas Eve, Scrooge learns that indeed the "common welfare" of all mankind is everyone's business. Through the intervention of his former partner, Jacob Marley, and three Ghosts, Scrooge learns to redefine "business" as more than a series of commercial transactions: "Mankind was my business. The common welfare was my business; charity, mercy, forbearance, and benevolence were all my business. The dealings of my trade were but a drop of water in the comprehensive ocean of my business!" (page 22).

As we'll see, once Scrooge discovers the cause of his own pathological cupidity, then and only then can he overcome it. He has to undergo a conversion experience—and therefore the emphasis at the beginning of the work on Scrooge's intractability and parsimoniousness is essential. In *Payback: Debt and The Shadow Side of Wealth*, Margaret Atwood argues that one of the reasons Scrooge endures as a character is because "true to the laws of wish-fulfillment, which always involve a free lunch or a get-out-of-jail-free card, he embodies both sides of the equation—the greedy getting and the gleeful spending—and comes out just fine" (page 98).

Ultimately, the effect of embracing common experience is to illuminate another passage from the Bible: Ecclesiastes 8:15. By the end of *A Christmas Carol*, Scrooge will be the embodiment of "Mirth, because a man hath no better thing under the sun, than to eat, and to drink, and to be merry." When Scrooge is able to release himself from his oppressive isolation and obsessive need to hoard money, his "own heart laughed" (page 105).

Dickens reassures us that the emotional, spiritual, and psychological work will be worth it: even when one is out of practice, as Scrooge had been, it is possible to have a "splendid laugh, a most illustrious laugh" which can become "the father of a long, long line of brilliant laughs!" (page 98).

It was neither joy nor satisfaction, however, which

prompted Dickens to write the first of his Christmas books. *A Christmas Carol* actually began life as a nonfiction project: a pamphlet to be titled "An appeal to the People of England on behalf of the Poor Man's Child" written as an amplification of *The Second Report (Trades and Manufactures) of the Children's Employment Commission* by social reformer Dr. Thomas Southwood Smith. According to Fred Guida's *A Christmas Carol and Its Adaptations*, Dickens was "appalled and infuriated by its descriptions of the horrible conditions in which young children were being forced to work" and initially conceived the idea of a pamphlet as a good way of drawing attention to their plight. But soon after, Dickens wrote to Smith with a change of plans, saying he had "reasons . . . for deferring the production of that pamphlet until the end of the year. I am not at liberty to explain them further, just now; but *rest assured* that when you know them, and see what I do, and where, and how, you will certainly feel that a Sledge hammer has come down with twenty times the force—twenty thousand times the force—I could exert by following out my first idea" (pages 28–29).

Also in October, and at the suggestion of one of his patrons, Dickens paid a visit to one of London's so-called "Ragged Schools" in one of the city's most vicious slums. Only the most destitute children from the most desperate situations were swept into these institutions, run by Evangelicals who offered Scripture along with the most basic forms of education. Dickens—no stranger to misery and poverty himself—was deeply disturbed by what he saw. In Michael Slater's definitive biography of Dickens, we learn that Dickens said he had "'very seldom seen . . . anything so shocking as the dire neglect of soul and body exhibited in these children.'" As Slater points out, Dickens regarded the experience as both shocking and ominous: "'In the prodigious misery and ignorance of the swarming masses of mankind in England, the seeds of its certain ruin are sown.' Within a month or so of writing this, Dickens would be creating those two child-monsters, 'horrible and dread,' Ignorance and Want, whose apparition, 'yellow, meager, ragged, scowling, wolfish,' so appalls Scrooge" (page 217)

Dickens wrote *A Christmas Carol* purposefully and swiftly. Beginning in October, and completing the book in time for what we would now call "the holiday rush," Dickens wove together a complex web of fantasy, fairy tale, and nightmare that continues to grasp our imagination as fully as it did when it appeared on December 19, 1843. The first printing of the book—an edition financed by Dickens himself—sold out almost immediately. It has, since the day of its publication, never been out of print.

It is now impossible, of course, to find either reader or critic foolish enough to believe Dickens would have done more good with a pamphlet urging social concern than he did by creating Bob Cratchit and Tiny Tim, or by embodying Ignorance and Want as the starving, feral offspring of London's slums. By making the issues into characters, by turning "The Poor" into "this poor child" and by putting faces onto the faceless, nameless bands of the unemployed and homeless, Dickens prompted an outpouring of charity by tapping into a wellspring of compassion. On December 26, 1843, Lord Jeffrey Cockburn wrote his friend Dickens a reassuring, celebratory note, saying, "[Y]ou may be sure you have done more good, and not only fastened more kindly feelings, but prompted more prominent acts of beneficence, by this little publication, than can be traced to all the pulpits and confessionals in Christendom, since Christmas 1842" (in Collins, page 149).

Why, even two hundred years since the birth of its author, does *A Christmas Carol* have such an enduring presence?

Many adaptations attempt to satisfy an audience by reducing the number of complicated psychological over-tones, transforming Scrooge into a kind of misguided practitioner of Conservative or Libertarian politics or a man more misunderstood than willfully miscreant.

The audience, however, knows better than to accept these salvos or salves. For Scrooge to be fully reclaimed, he must be fully lost; for the story to work, the charac-ter of Scrooge must be as close to evil as anyone can be—anyone, that is, who can expect not only the chilly chastisement of contrition accepted but the warm em-brace of mercy and reconciliation offered.

Even as Jacob Marley must be proven dead—"dead as a door-nail" with "register of burial signed by the clergyman"(page 3)—for the ghost story to achieve the right level of frisson and spookiness, so must Scrooge be convincingly ruthless and flinty for the story of his salvation to achieve authenticity. This is more than your ordinary knock-knock joke, after all. Jacob Mar-ley needs to refute Scrooge's taunt, "You may be an undigested bit of beef, a blot of mustard, a crumb of cheese, a fragment of an underdone potato. There's more of gravy than of grave about you, whatever you are!" (page 19), and Scrooge needs to be more than just a grumpy old man.

Therefore the book, comic as it is, must establish its level of seriousness early. It does this when Marley shows Scrooge that he is not the only ghost lingering in London that night, but that the "air was filled with phantoms, wandering hither and thither in restless haste, and moaning as they went. . . . Many had been personally known to Scrooge in their lives. He had been quite familiar with one old ghost, in a white waistcoat, with a monstrous iron safe attached to his ankle, who cried piteously at being unable to assist a wretched woman with an infant, whom he saw below, upon a doorstep. The misery with them all was, clearly, that they sought to interfere, for good, in human matters, and had lost the power forever" (page 25).

A number of critics regard Jacob Marley's contrition as a kind of "contagion for good"—a sort of health that can be spread by spiritual contact. Scrooge "catches" it in time and becomes immune to the kind of damnation experienced by his former business partner. And as Eileen Gillooly and Deirdre David note in *Contemporary Dickens*, the spiritual, the physical, and the fiscal overlap in *Carol*: "In a kind of trickle-down theory of salvation, Marley saves Scrooge from the eternal damnation of liberal guilt by making him temporally (and temporarily) guilty so that he can, in turn, save Tiny Tim's life and the rest of the Cratchits from material want (their souls, after all, are not in danger)" (page 124).

Both supernatural and emotional subtleties characterize the work, and Dickens brilliantly choreographs their interplay. The author is creator, character, analyst, and critic; Dickens's own instinctive understanding of human nature simply presages Freud. Sigmund Freud, of course, envied the poets and writers who understood human nature instinctively and did almost automatically in their art what he did so painstakingly in his science ("If we could at least discover in ourselves . . . an activity which was in some way akin to creative writing!" laments the father of psychoanalysis in *Creative Writers and Daydreaming*).

In *A Christmas Carol,* Dickens holds high the candle whose light Freud will reflect decades later: Dickens provided ample fodder for a Freudian reading (being of the devil's party without knowing it, perhaps?) by his emphasis on the following points: 1. To understand Scrooge we must have insight into the reasons for his behavior, which are repressed and which stem from his childhood; 2. For Scrooge to alter his behavior in the present and change patterns of behavior for the future, he must come to grips with suppressed memories, old emotions, and hidden motivations; 3. He cannot do this on his own, but must receive professional help—in his case, from the ghost of his former business partner, Jacob Marley, and the Spirits of Christmas Past, Christmas Present, and Christmas Future; 4. Like all good analysts, Marley and the Christmas Ghosts force Scrooge to review his past and to restructure both his vocabulary and his perspective.

To break it down even further, the Ghost of Christmas Past permits Scrooge to come to terms with his Id (his most infantile self, the instinctive unmediated part that desires, needs, and fears most fundamentally); Christmas Present aids Scrooge with his Ego (the part of the self that deals with reality, with the everyday, with immediate circumstances); and Christmas Future permits Scrooge to internalize and engage his Super-Ego (the ethical and moral self, the conscience, the internalized judge and jury).

I'm not alone in seeing the ghost of analysts-yet-to-come in *Carol: The New York Times*'s annual review of the 1951 classic British adaptation (for many, its star, Alistair Sim, remains the quintessential Scrooge) describes the film as "heavy on the Freudian Sauce." Yet it is important to understand that the "Freudian Sauce" is drawn from the text itself without any filmic additions or heavy-handed spicing up.

Just as an analyst might encourage a client to examine the most significant events shaping his childhood, to review his present circumstances, and to understand how his idiosyncrasies could affect his future, so do the Spirits of Christmas encourage Scrooge to take account of his life with the same scrutiny he has thus far brought only to his bank ledger.

Like the best of analysts, the Ghosts allow Scrooge to do most of the talking. They present him with incidents, call up memories, and solicit reactions; but just as Marley has to carry the full weight of "the chains [he] forged in life," so will Scrooge have to do the emotional heavy lifting in order to "make amends for one life's opportunities misused" (pages 21–22).

And so we see that the key points in each scene occur when Scrooge speaks unself-consciously or on behalf of his "former self," beginning with the Ghost of Christmas Past.

As the first of the Christmas Ghosts to visit Scrooge, it is incumbent upon the Ghost of Christmas Past to make Ebenezer remember the neglected child he had once been. Scrooge must experience the pain of his own abandonment in order to begin the process of thawing out his frozen emotional life. The Ghost shows Scrooge a dreary institution, "a large house, but one of broken fortunes," emptied of its charges because families have fetched their children home for the holiday. Yet "[t]he school is not quite deserted," points out the

Ghost. "A solitary child, neglected by his friends, is left there still." Scrooge says he knows it. "And he sobbed" (page 33).

By being able to weep when he looks upon "his poor forgotten self as he had used to be" and to be able to exclaim "Poor boy!" in sincere pity (page 34), Scrooge begins to reclaim his connection to humanity. Only by being able to reclaim a connection to his own younger self, however, can this connection to any sense of community be accomplished.

The Victorians, argues Daniel Born in *The Birth of Liberal Guilt in the English Novel*, needed to feel the "weight" of responsibility for more than their own lives, however; members of the growing middle and upper-middle classes must, Born argues, develop an increasing sense of individual "obligation to help bring [an ethical social order] into being. Hope turns to duty; utopian visions turn to guilt; the residue after the mopping up of spilt religion goes from sweet to sour" (page 29). Not only does Dickens "want to apportion responsibility for wasted and tragic lives," insists Born, but he also rejects the standard Victorian moralism by his "willingness to assign blame not only to individual profligacy, but also, and more aggressively so, to the powerful, the privileged and the callous who make the social rules; read here: middle-class agency, middle-class complicity" (page 35).

And if the scenes with the very young Ebenezer are particularly intense and emotionally raw, many critics have argued that Dickens's own childhood experiences inform them. Late in his life, Dickens wrote that in his own youth, "no one had compassion enough on me—a child of singular abilities, quick, eager, delicate, and soon hurt, bodily or mentally" (Parker, page 174). Taken out of school when his father was imprisoned in the Marshalsea debtors' jail and forced into miserable work at Warren's Blacking Warehouse, Dickens would later describe that part of his life as "the secret agony of my soul." His friend John Foster, author of *The Life of Charles Dickens*, which was published in 1870 right after Dickens's death, records Dickens's description of Warren's as follows:

> The blacking-warehouse was the last house on the left-hand side of the way, at old Hungerford Stairs. It was a crazy, tumble-down old house, abutting of course on the river, and literally overrun with rats. Its wainscoted rooms, and its rotten floors and staircase, and the old grey rats swarming down in the cellars, and the sound of their squeaking and scuffling coming up the stairs at all times, and the dirt and decay of the place, rise up visibly before me, as if I were there again.   (Foster, xx)

No wonder the man looking back on the child wept, "Poor boy!" Yet only after Scrooge laments a second time about the child he once was—crying "Poor boy!" again—is he able to shift his empathy to another person entirely. Only by recognizing, witnessing, and experiencing the depth of his own pain is he able to commiserate with others.

And thus Scrooge is able to speak sincerely, and without his signature bravado or defensiveness, two sentences that offer the first glimpse of what will become authentic emotional engagement; when Scrooge mutters, "There was a boy singing a Christmas carol at my door last night. I should like to have given him something" (page 35), he takes a small but irrevocable step back into the world of a living, breathing, even welcoming humanity.

Even if he would not be able to define it as such, Scrooge discovers that pity is found to be a transferable commodity: it can move from the self to the other—from Scrooge to a nameless boy who, "gnawed and mumbled by the hungry cold as bones are gnawed by dogs" (page 12), attempted to sing "God Rest Ye, Merry Gentlemen" and was driven from the door by Scrooge in a fit of wrath. Once Scrooge discovers a wellspring of pity, he sees that it flows freely and that it is also accompanied by other forces and emotions: compassion, forbearance, pleasure, mercy—and regret. He regrets losing the woman he once loved, who released him from their engagement because she was a "dowerless girl" who understood that her once-beloved Ebenezer was a changed man; he now "weigh[ed] everything by Gain" and would never have chosen her were he free (page 44). He regrets losing what had once been a considerable talent for fun, cultivated when he worked as an apprentice to the Fezziwigs. Observing the Fezziwigs with the Ghost, Scrooge acts "like a man out of his wits" and behaves like his "former self" (page 41). He forgets the very presence of the Ghost in his enjoyment of the scene. The Ghost points out to Scrooge that it was a small matter for Fezziwig "to make these silly folks so full of gratitude.... He has spent but a few pounds of your mortal money: three or four, perhaps. Is that so much that he deserves this praise," to which Scooge "heatedly" replies, "It isn't that, Spirit.... The happiness he gives, is quite as great as if it cost a fortune" (pages 41–42).

As the rest of the novel progresses, the Spirits encourage Scrooge to change his life by understanding the reasons why he acts the way he does, and to understand that his present judgments are based on old information. By providing him with the experiences permitting him to draw his own conclusions, Scrooge learns that in everything he does, from the disdainful banishment of his nephew to the unnecessarily shoddy trappings in which he lives every day of his own life, is an unconscious reaction to the past.

And so it is through a "talking cure" offered by the Spirits that Scrooge's conversion is made possible. The conversion is secular rather than religious: Scrooge must see the world around him, with an implication that heaven can wait.

In perhaps the single most significant scene in the novel, the Ghost of Christmas Present displays for Scrooge two small children, described as "wretched, abject, frightful, hideous, miserable." They have been concealed beneath his gown until Scrooge asks what the Ghost has been hiding. In a scene of rather theatrical reveal, we see:

> a boy and girl. Yellow, meager, ragged, scowling, wolfish; but prostrate, too, in their humility. Where graceful youth should have filled their features out, and touched them with its freshest tints, a stale and shriveled hand, like that of age, had pinched and twisted them, and pulled them into shreds. Where angels might have sat enthroned, devils lurked, and glared out menacing. . . . "This boy is Ignorance. This girl is Want. Beware of them both, and all of their degree, but most of all beware of this boy."
>
> (pages 75–76)

Their next exchange illustrates how far Scrooge has come through the administration of the Spirits. When, in genuine distress, he begs, "Have they no refuge or resource?" the Spirit—once again, like a good analyst—uses Scrooges own words to help him understand. "Are there no prisons?" says the Spirit, turning on him for the last time with his own words. "Are there no work-houses?" (page 76).

Scrooge begins the book as a man who fears humiliation and ends it as a man who embraces humility. Humility, he learns, is a virtue. To be of service, he learns, is a vocation.

By the end of the long night, Scrooge dares not ask the final Ghost for words, but supplies them himself. He faces and then answers the silence. He can bear what's spoken and address what is left unsaid.

When he wakes up to find that the Spirits have given him short shrift, taking less time to complete the process than he'd been warned—("The Spirits have done it all in one night. They can do anything they like. Of course they can. Of course they can" [page 99])—and completing his makeover in one night rather than in three, he accepts the gift with the kind of childlike gratitude that only a humble heart can offer. (The fact that the Ghosts complete the process all at once is rather like the fact that *A Christmas Carol* appeared all at once, and not in the usual piecemeal serialized form.) And once again we see the effects of contagion: only this time, happiness and a sense of abundance are being passed from one household to another, with Scrooge as carrier and host.

The fact that Scrooge has thrown off all shame, guilt, and selfishness is no more evident than in these, some of the final lines of the story, where Ebenezer is now spiritually and emotionally healthy enough to resist the effects of the mockery he'll receive from those who will not accept his changed life. Immune to their ridicule and disbelief, he is invulnerable precisely because of his renewed sense of openness. His laughter, finally, is a joyful symptom of his wholeness and the very sound of it is almost as good as a poor child singing "God Rest Ye, Merry Gentlemen" through the cold night's fog:

> Some people laughed to see the alteration in him, but he let them laugh, and little heeded them, for he was wise enough to know that nothing ever happened on this globe, for good, at which some people did not have their fill of laughter in the outset; and knowing that such as these would be blind anyway, he thought it quite as well that they should wrinkle up their eyes in grins, as have the malady in less attractive forms. His own heart laughed, and that was quite enough for him. (pages 104–5)

—Regina Barreca

A
Christmas Carol
and Other Christmas Stories

A Christmas Carol

❦❦❦❦❦❦❦❦❦❦❦❦❦❦

STAVE ONE

Marley's Ghost

Marley was dead, to begin with. There is no doubt whatever about that. The register of his burial was signed by the clergyman, the clerk, the undertaker, and the chief mourner. Scrooge signed it. And Scrooge's name was good upon 'Change for anything he chose to put his hand to.

Old Marley was as dead as a door-nail.

Mind! I don't mean to say that I know, of my own knowledge, what there is particularly dead about a door-nail. I might have been inclined, myself, to regard a coffin-nail as the deadest piece of ironmongery in the trade. But the wisdom of our ancestors is in the simile; and my unhallowed hands shall not disturb it, or the Country's done for. You will therefore permit me to repeat, emphatically, that Marley was as dead as a door-nail.

Scrooge knew he was dead? Of course he did. How could it be otherwise? Scrooge and he were partners for I don't know how many years. Scrooge was his sole executor, his sole administrator, his sole assign, his sole rosiduary legatee, his sole friend, and sole mourner. And even Scrooge was not so dreadfully cut up by the sad event, but that he was an excellent man of business on the very day of the funeral, and solemnized it with an undoubted bargain.

The mention of Marley's funeral brings me back to the point I started from. There is no doubt that Marley was dead. This must be distinctly understood, or nothing wonderful can come of the story I am going to relate. If we were not perfectly convinced that Hamlet's father died before the play began, there would be nothing more remarkable in his taking a stroll at night, in an easterly wind, upon his own ramparts, than there would be in any other middle-aged gentleman rashly turning out after dark in a breezy spot—say Saint Paul's Churchyard for instance—literally to astonish his son's weak mind.

Scrooge never painted out old Marley's name. There it stood, years afterward, above the warehouse door; Scrooge and Marley. The firm was known as Scrooge and Marley. Sometimes people new to the business called Scrooge Scrooge, and sometimes Marley, but he answered to both names. It was all the same to him.

Oh! but he was a tight-fisted hand at the grindstone, Scrooge! a squeezing, wrenching, grasping, scraping, clutching, covetous old sinner! Hard and sharp as flint, from which no steel had ever struck out generous fire, secret, and self-contained, and solitary as an oyster. The cold within him froze his old features, nipped his pointed nose, shriveled his cheek, stiffened his gait, made his eyes red, his thin lips blue, and spoke out shrewdly in his grating voice. A frosty rime was on his head, and on his eyebrows, and his wiry chin. He carried his own low temperature always about with him;

he iced his office in the dog-days; and didn't thaw it one degree at Christmas.

External heat and cold had little influence on Scrooge. No warmth could warm, no wintry weather chill him. No wind that blew was bitterer than he, no falling snow was more intent upon its purpose, no pelting rain less open to entreaty. Foul weather didn't know where to have him. The heaviest rain, and snow, and hail, and sleet, could boast of the advantage over him in only one respect. They often "came down" handsomely, and Scrooge never did.

Nobody ever stopped him in the street to say, with gladsome looks, "My dear Scrooge, how are you? When will you come to see me?" No beggars implored him to bestow a trifle, no children asked him what it was o'clock, no man or woman ever once in all his life inquired the way to such and such a place, of Scrooge. Even the blind men's dogs appeared to know him; and, when they saw him coming on, would tug their owners into doorways and up courts; and then would wag their tails as though they said, "No eye at all is better than an evil eye, dark master!"

But what did Scrooge care? It was the very thing he liked. To edge his way along the crowded paths of life, warning all human sympathy to keep its distance, was what the knowing ones call "nuts" to Scrooge.

Once upon a time—of all the good days in the year, on Christmas Eve—old Scrooge sat busy in his counting-house. It was cold, bleak, biting weather, foggy withal, and he could hear the people in the court outside go wheezing up and down, beating their hands upon their breasts, and stamping their feet upon the pavement stones to warm them. The city clocks had only just gone three, but it was quite dark already—it had

not been light all day—and candles were flaring in the
windows of the neighboring offices, like ruddy smears
upon the palpable brown air. The fog came pouring in
at every chink and keyhole, and was so dense without, that, although the court was of the narrowest, the
houses opposite were mere phantoms. To see the dingy
cloud come drooping down, obscuring everything, one
might have thought that Nature lived hard by, and was
brewing on a large scale.

The door of Scrooge's counting-house was open,
that he might keep his eye upon his clerk, who, in a
dismal little cell beyond, a sort of tank, was copying
letters. Scrooge had a very small fire, but the clerk's fire
was so very much smaller that it looked like one coal.
But he couldn't replenish it, for Scrooge kept the coal-
box in his own room; and so surely as the clerk came
in with the shovel, the master predicted that it would
be necessary for them to part. Wherefore the clerk put
on his white comforter, and tried to warm himself at
the candle; in which effort, not being a man of a strong
imagination, he failed.

"A merry Christmas, uncle! God save you!" cried a
cheerful voice. It was the voice of Scrooge's nephew,
who came upon him so quickly that this was the first
intimation he had of his approach.

"Bah!" said Scrooge. "Humbug!"

He had so heated himself with rapid walking in the
fog and frost, this nephew of Scrooge's, that he was all
in a glow; his face was ruddy and handsome; his eyes
sparkled, and his breath smoked again.

"Christmas a humbug, uncle!" said Scrooge's nephew.
"You don't mean that, I am sure?"

"I do," said Scrooge. "Merry Christmas! What right

have you to be merry? What reason have you to be merry? You're poor enough."

"Come, then," returned the nephew gaily. "What right have you to be dismal? What reason have you to be morose? You're rich enough."

Scrooge, having no better answer ready on the spur of the moment, said "Bah!" again; and followed it up with "Humbug!"

"Don't be cross, uncle!" said the nephew.

"What else can I be," returned the uncle, "when I live in such a world of fools as this? Merry Christmas! Out upon merry Christmas! What's Christmas-time to you but a time for paying bills without money; a time for finding yourself a year older, and not an hour richer; a time for balancing your books, and having every item in 'em through a round dozen of months presented dead against you? If I could work my will," said Scrooge indignantly, "every idiot who goes about with 'Merry Christmas' on his lips should be boiled with his own pudding, and buried with a stake of holly through his heart. He should!"

"Uncle!" pleaded the nephew.

"Nephew!" returned the uncle sternly, "keep Christmas in your own way, and let me keep it in mine."

"Keep it!" repeated Scrooge's nephew. "But you don't keep it."

"Let me leave it alone, then," said Scrooge. "Much good may it do you! Much good it has ever done you!"

"There are many things from which I might have derived good by which I have not profited, I dare say," returned the nephew, "Christmas among the rest. But I am sure I have always thought of Christmas-time,

when it has come round—apart from the veneration
due to its sacred name and origin, if anything belonging to it can be apart from that—as a good time; a kind,
forgiving, charitable, pleasant time; the only time I
know of, in the long calendar of the year, when men
and women seem by one consent to open their shut-up
hearts freely, and to think of people below them as if
they really were fellow-passengers to the grave, and
not another race of creatures bound on other journeys.
And therefore, uncle, though it has never put a scrap
of gold or silver in my pocket, I believe that it *has* done
me good, and *will* do me good; and I say, God bless
it!"

The clerk in the tank involuntarily applauded. Becoming immediately sensible of the impropriety, he
poked the fire, and extinguished the last frail spark
forever.

"Let me hear another sound from *you*," said Scrooge,
"and you'll keep your Christmas by losing your situation! You're quite a powerful speaker, sir," he added,
turning to his nephew. "I wonder you don't go into
Parliament."

"Don't be angry, uncle. Come! Dine with us to-
morrow."

Scrooge said that he would see him—Yes, indeed,
he did. He went the whole length of the expression,
and said that he would see him in that extremity first.

"But why?" cried Scrooge's nephew. "Why?"

"Why did you get married?" said Scrooge.

"Because I fell in love."

"Because you fell in love!" growled Scrooge, as if
that were the only one thing in the world more ridiculous than a merry Christmas. "Good afternoon!"

"Nay, uncle, but you never came to see me before

that happened. Why give it as a reason for not coming now?"

"Good afternoon," said Scrooge.

"I want nothing from you; I ask nothing of you; why cannot we be friends?"

"Good afternoon!" said Scrooge.

"I am sorry, with all my heart, to find you so resolute. We have never had any quarrel, to which I have been a party. But I have made the trial in homage to Christmas, and I'll keep my Christmas humor to the last. So a merry Christmas, uncle!"

"Good afternoon," said Scrooge.

"And a happy New Year!"

"Good afternoon!" said Scrooge.

His nephew left the room without an angry word, notwithstanding. He stopped at the outer door to bestow the greetings of the season on the clerk, who, cold as he was, was warmer than Scrooge, for he returned them cordially.

"There's another fellow," muttered Scrooge, who overheard him; "my clerk, with fifteen shillings a week, and a wife and family, talking about a merry Christmas. I'll retire to Bedlam."

This lunatic, in letting Scrooge's nephew out, had let two other people in. They were portly gentlemen, pleasant to behold, and now stood with their hats off, in Scrooge's office. They had books and papers in their hands, and bowed to him.

"Scrooge and Marley's, I believe," said one of the gentlemen, referring to his list. "Have I the pleasure of addressing Mr. Scrooge, or Mr. Marley?"

"Mr. Marley has been dead these seven years," Scrooge replied. "He died seven years ago, this very night."

"We have no doubt his liberality is well represented by his surviving partner," said the gentleman, presenting his credentials.

It certainly was; for they had been two kindred spirits. At the ominous word "liberality," Scrooge frowned, and shook his head, and handed the credentials back.

"At this festive season of the year, Mr. Scrooge," said the gentleman, taking up a pen, "it is more than usually desirable that we should make some slight provision for the poor and destitute, who suffer greatly at the present time. Many thousands are in want of common necessaries; hundreds of thousands are in want of common comforts, sir."

"Are there no prisons?" asked Scrooge.

"Plenty of prisons," said the gentleman, laying down the pen again.

"And the Union workhouses?" demanded Scrooge. "Are they still in operation?"

"They are. Still," returned the gentleman, "I wish I could say they were not."

"The Treadmill and the Poor Law are in full vigor, then?" said Scrooge.

"Both very busy, sir."

"Oh! I was afraid, from what you said at first, that something had occurred to stop them in their useful course," said Scrooge. "I'm very glad to hear it."

"Under the impression that they scarcely furnish Christian cheer of mind or body to the multitude," returned the gentleman, "a few of us are endeavoring to raise a fund to buy the poor some meat and drink, and means of warmth. We choose this time, because it is a time, of all others, when Want is keenly felt, and Abundance rejoices. What shall I put you down for?"

"Nothing!" Scrooge replied.

"You wish to be anonymous?"

"I wish to be left alone," said Scrooge. "Since you ask me what I wish, gentlemen, that is my answer. I don't make merry myself at Christmas, and I can't afford to make idle people merry. I help to support the establishments I have mentioned—they cost enough; and those who are badly off must go there."

"Many can't go there; and many would rather die."

"If they would rather die," said Scrooge, "they had better do it, and decrease the surplus population. Besides—excuse me—I don't know that."

"But you might know it," observed the gentleman.

"It's not my business," Scrooge returned. "It's enough for a man to understand his own business, and not to interfere with other people's. Mine occupies me constantly. Good afternoon, gentlemen!"

Seeing clearly that it would be useless to pursue their point, the gentlemen withdrew. Scrooge resumed his labors with an improved opinion of himself, and in a more facetious temper than was usual with him.

Meanwhile the fog and darkness thickened so that people ran about with flaring links, proffering their services to go before horses in carriages, and conduct them on their way. The ancient tower of a church, whose gruff old bell was always peeping slyly down at Scrooge out of a Gothic window in the wall, became invisible, and struck the hours and quarters in the clouds, with tremulous vibrations afterward, as if its teeth were chattering in its frozen head up there. The cold became intense. In the main street, at the corner of the court, some laborers were repairing the gaspipes, and had lighted a great fire in a brazier, round which a party of ragged men and boys were gathered, warming their hands and winking their eyes before the blaze, in rapture. The water-plug being left in solitude, its overflowings suddenly congealed, and turned to misanthropic ice. The brightness of the shops, where holly sprigs and berries crackled in the lamp heat of the windows, made pale faces ruddy as they passed. Poulterers' and grocers' trades became a splendid joke; a glorious pageant, with which it was next to impossible to believe that such dull principles as bargain and sale had anything to do. The Lord Mayor, in the stronghold of the mighty Mansion House, gave orders to his fifty cooks and butlers to keep Christmas as a Lord Mayor's household should; and even the little tailor, whom he had fined five shillings on the previous Monday for being drunk and bloodthirsty in the streets, stirred up to-morrow's pudding in his garret, while his lean wife and baby sallied out to buy the beef.

Foggier yet, and colder! Piercing, searching, biting cold. If the good Saint Dunstan had but nipped the Evil Spirit's nose with a touch of such weather as that, instead of using his familiar weapons, then, indeed, he would have roared to lusty purpose. The owner of one scant young nose, gnawed and mumbled by the hungry cold as bones are gnawed by dogs, stooped down at Scrooge's keyhole to regale him with a Christmas carol; but at the first sound of

> God rest you, merry gentleman,
> May nothing you dismay,

Scrooge seized the ruler with such energy of action, that the singer fled in terror, leaving the keyhole to the fog and even more congenial frost.

At length the hour of shutting up the counting-house arrived. With an ill will Scrooge dismounted from his stool, and tacitly admitted the fact to the expectant clerk in the tank, who instantly snuffed his candle out, and put on his hat.

"You'll want all day to-morrow, I suppose?" said Scrooge.

"If quite convenient, sir."

"It's not convenient," said Scrooge, "and it's not fair. If I was to stop half a crown for it, you'd think yourself ill used, I'll be bound?"

The clerk smiled faintly.

"And yet," said Scrooge, "you don't think *me* ill used when I pay a day's wages for no work."

The clerk observed that it was only once a year.

"A poor excuse for picking a man's pocket every twenty-fifth of December!" said Scrooge, buttoning his greatcoat to the chin. "But I suppose you must have the whole day. Be here all the earlier next morning."

The clerk promised that he would; and Scrooge walked out with a growl. The office was closed in a twinkling, and the clerk, with the long ends of his white comforter dangling below his waist (for he boasted no greatcoat), went down a slide on Cornhill, at the end of a lane of boys, twenty times, in honor of its being Christmas Eve, and then ran home to Camden Town, as hard as he could pelt, to play at blindman's buff.

Scrooge took his melancholy dinner in his usual melancholy tavern; and having read all the newspapers, and beguiled the rest of the evening with his banker's book, went home to bed. He lived in chambers which had once belonged to his deceased partner. They were a gloomy suite of rooms, in a lowering pile of building up a yard, where it had so little business to be, that one could scarcely help fancying it must have run there when it was a young house, playing at hide-and-seek with other houses, and have forgotten the way out again. It was old enough now, and dreary enough, for nobody lived in it but Scrooge, the other rooms being all let out as offices. The yard was so dark that even Scrooge, who knew its every stone, was fain to grope with his hands. The fog and frost so hung about the black old gateway of the house, that it seemed as if the Genius of the Weather sat in mournful meditation on the threshold.

Now it is a fact that there was nothing at all particular about the knocker on the door, except that it was very large. It is also a fact that Scrooge had seen it, night and morning, during his whole residence in that place; also that Scrooge had as little of what is called fancy about him as any man in the City of London, even including—which is a bold word—the corporation, aldermen, and livery. Let it also be borne in mind that Scrooge had not bestowed one thought on Marley, since his last mention of his seven-years-dead partner that afternoon. And then let any man explain to me, if he can, how it happened that Scrooge, having his key in the lock of the door, saw in the knocker, without its undergoing any intermediate process of change—not a knocker, but Marley's face.

Marley's face. It was not in impenetrable shadow, as the other objects in the yard were, but had a dismal light about it, like a bad lobster in a dark cellar. It was not angry or ferocious, but looked at Scrooge as Marley used to look: with ghostly spectacles turned up on its ghostly forehead. The hair was curiously stirred, as if by breath or hot air; and though the eyes were wide open, they were perfectly motionless. That, and its livid color, made it horrible; but its horror seemed to be in spite of the face, and beyond its control, rather than a part of its own expression.

As Scrooge looked fixedly at this phenomenon it was a knocker again.

To say that he was not startled, or that his blood was not conscious of a terrible sensation to which it had been a stranger from infancy, would be untrue. But he put his hand upon the key he had relinquished, turned it sturdily, walked in, and lighted his candle.

He *did* pause, with a moment's irresolution, before he shut the door; and he *did* look cautiously behind it first, as if he half expected to be terrified with the sight of Marley's pigtail sticking out into the hall. But there was nothing on the back of the door, except the screws and nuts that held the knocker on, so he said, "Pooh, pooh!" and closed it with a bang.

The sound resounded through the house like thunder. Every room above, and every cask in the wine-merchant's cellars below, appeared to have a separate peal of echoes of its own. Scrooge was not a man to be frightened by echoes. He fastened the door, and walked across the hall, and up the stairs, slowly, too, trimming his candle as he went.

You may talk vaguely about driving a coach and six up a good old flight of stairs, or through a bad young Act of Parliament; but I mean to say you might have got a hearse up that staircase, and taken it broadwise, with the splinter-bar toward the wall, and the door toward the balustrades, and done it easy. There was plenty of width for that, and room to spare; which is perhaps the reason why Scrooge thought he saw a locomotive hearse going on before him in the gloom. Half a dozen gas-lamps out of the street wouldn't have lighted the entry too well, so you may suppose that it was pretty dark with Scrooge's dip.

Up Scrooge went, not caring a button for that. Dark-

ness is cheap, and Scrooge liked it. But before he shut
his heavy door, he walked through his rooms to see
that all was right. He had just enough recollection of
the face to desire to do that.

Sitting-room, bedroom, lumber-room. All as they
should be. Nobody under the table, nobody under the
sofa; a small fire in the grate; spoon and basin ready;
and the little saucepan of gruel (Scrooge had a cold
in his head) upon the hob. Nobody under the bed;
nobody in the closet; nobody in his dressing-gown,
which was hanging up in a suspicious attitude against
the wall. Lumber-room as usual. Old fire-guard, old
shoes, two fish-baskets, washing-stand on three legs,
and a poker.

Quite satisfied, he closed his door, and locked himself
in; double-locked himself in, which was not his custom.
Thus secured against surprise, he took off his cravat, put
on his dressing-gown and slippers, and his night-cap,
and sat down before the fire to take his gruel.

It was a very low fire indeed; nothing on such a bitter night. He was obliged to sit close to it, and brood
over it, before he could extract the least sensation of
warmth from such a handful of fuel. The fireplace was
an old one, built by some Dutch merchant long ago,
and paved all round with quaint Dutch tiles, designed
to illustrate the Scriptures. There were Cains and
Abels, Pharaoh's daughters, Queens of Sheba, angelic
messengers descending through the air on clouds like
feather-beds, Abrahams, Belshazzars, Apostles putting
off to sea in butter-boats, hundreds of figures to attract
his thoughts; and yet that face of Marley, seven years
dead, came like the ancient Prophet's rod, and swallowed up the whole. If each smooth tile had been a
blank at first, with power to shape some picture on its

surface from the disjointed fragments of his thoughts, there would have been a copy of old Marley's head on every one.

"Humbug!" said Scrooge; and walked across the room.

After several turns, he sat down again. As he threw his head back in the chair, his glance happened to rest upon a bell, a disused bell, that hung in the room, and communicated, for some purpose now forgotten, with a chamber in the highest story of the building. It was with great astonishment, and with a strange, inexplicable dread, that, as he looked, he saw this bell begin to swing. It swung so softly in the outset that it scarcely made a sound; but soon it rang out loudly, and so did every bell in the house.

This might have lasted half a minute, or a minute, but it seemed an hour. The bells ceased, as they had begun, together. They were succeeded by a clanking noise, deep down below; as if some person were dragging a heavy chain over the casks in the wine-merchant's cellar. Scrooge then remembered to have heard that ghosts in haunted houses were described as dragging chains.

The cellar door flew open with a booming sound, and then he heard the noise, much louder, on the floors below; then coming up the stairs; then coming straight toward his door.

"It's humbug still!" said Scrooge. "I won't believe it!"

His color changed, though, when, without a pause, it came on through the heavy door, and passed into the room before his eyes. Upon its coming in, the dying flame leaped up, as though it cried, "I know him! Marley's Ghost!" and fell again.

The same face, the very same. Marley, in his pigtail, usual waistcoat, tights and boots; the tassels on the latter bristling like his pigtail, and his coat-skirts, and the hair upon his head. The chain he drew was clasped about his middle. It was long, and wound about him like a tail; and it was made (for Scrooge observed it closely) of cash-boxes, keys, padlocks, ledgers, deeds, and heavy purses wrought in steel. His body was transparent; so that Scrooge, observing him, and looking through his waistcoat, could see the two buttons on his coat behind.

Scrooge had often heard it said that Marley had no bowels, but he had never believed it until now.

No, nor did he believe it even now. Though he looked the phantom through and through, and saw it standing before him; though he felt the chilling influence of its death-cold eyes, and marked the very texture of the folded kerchief bound about its head and chin, which wrapper he had not observed before, he was still incredulous, and fought against his senses.

"How now!" said Scrooge, caustic and cold as ever. "What do you want with me?"

"Much!"—Marley's voice, no doubt about it.

"Who are you?"

"Ask me who I *was*."

"Who *were* you, then?" said Scrooge, raising his voice. "You're particular, for a shade." He was going to say, "*to* a shade," but substituted this, as more appropriate.

"In life I was your partner, Jacob Marley."

"Can you—can you sit down?" asked Scrooge, looking doubtfully at him.

"I can."

"Do it, then."

Scrooge asked the question, because he didn't know whether a ghost so transparent might find himself in a condition to take a chair; and felt in the event of its being impossible, it might involve the necessity of an embarrassing explanation. But the Ghost sat down on the opposite side of the fireplace, as if he were quite used to it.

"You don't believe in me," observed the Ghost.

"I don't," said Scrooge.

"What evidence would you have of my reality beyond that of your own senses?"

"I don't know," said Scrooge.

"Why do you doubt your senses?"

"Because," said Scrooge, "a little thing affects them. A slight disorder of the stomach makes them cheats. You may be an undigested bit of beef, a blot of mustard, a crumb of cheese, a fragment of an underdone potato. There's more of gravy than of grave about you, whatever you are!"

Scrooge was not much in the habit of cracking jokes, nor did he feel, in his heart, by any means waggish then. The truth is, that he tried to be smart, as a means of distracting his own attention, and keeping down his terror, for the specter's voice disturbed the very marrow in his bones.

To sit staring at those fixed glazed eyes in silence, for a moment, would play, Scrooge felt, the very deuce with him. There was something very awful, too, in the specter's being provided with an infernal atmosphere of his own. Scrooge could not feel it himself, but this was clearly the case; for though the Ghost sat perfectly motionless, his hair, and skirts, and tassels were still agitated as by the hot vapor from an oven.

"You see this toothpick?" said Scrooge, returning

quickly to the charge, for the reason just assigned; and wishing, though it were only for a second, to divert the vision's stony gaze from himself.

"I do," replied the Ghost.

"You are not looking at it," said Scrooge.

"But I see it," said the Ghost, "notwithstanding."

"Well!" returned Scrooge, "I have but to swallow this, and be for the rest of my days persecuted by a legion of goblins, all my own creation. Humbug, I tell you; humbug!"

At this the spirit raised a frightful cry, and shook his chain with such a dismal and appalling noise, that Scrooge held on tight to his chair, to save himself from falling in a swoon. But how much greater was his horror when, the phantom taking off the bandage round his head, as if it were too warm to wear indoors, his lower jaw dropped down upon his breast!

Scrooge fell upon his knees, and clasped his hands before his face.

"Mercy!" he said. "Dreadful apparition, why do you trouble me?"

"Man of the worldly mind!" replied the Ghost, "do you believe in me or not?"

"I do," said Scrooge. "I must. But why do spirits walk the earth, and why do they come to me?"

"It is required of every man," the Ghost returned, "that the spirit within him should walk abroad among his fellow-men, and travel far and wide; and if that spirit goes not forth in life, it is condemned to do so after death. It is doomed to wander through the world—oh, woe is me!—and witness what it cannot share, but might have shared on earth, and turned to happiness!"

Again the specter raised a cry, and shook his chain and wrung his shadowy hands.

"You are fettered," said Scrooge trembling. "Tell me why?"

"I wear the chain I forged in life," replied the Ghost. "I made it link by link, and yard by yard; I girded it on of my own free will, and of my own free will I wore it. Is its pattern strange to *you*?"

Scrooge trembled more and more.

"Or would you know," pursued the Ghost, "the weight and length of the strong coil you bear yourself? It was full as heavy and as long as this, seven Christmas Eves ago. You have labored on it, since. It is a ponderous chain!"

Scrooge glanced about him on the floor, in the expectation of finding himself surrounded by some fifty or sixty fathoms of iron cable; but he could see nothing.

"Jacob!" he said imploringly. "Old Jacob Marley, tell me more! Speak comfort to me, Jacob!"

"I have none to give," the Ghost replied. "It comes from other regions, Ebenezer Scrooge, and is conveyed by other ministers, to other kinds of men. Nor can I tell you what I would. A very little more is all permitted to me. I cannot rest, I cannot stay, I cannot linger anywhere. My spirit never walked beyond our counting-house—mark me!—in life my spirit never roved beyond the narrow limits of our money-changing hole; and weary journeys lie before me!"

It was a habit with Scrooge, whenever he became thoughtful, to put his hands in his breeches pockets. Pondering on what the Ghost had said, he did so now, but without lifting up his eyes, or getting off his knees.

"You must have been very slow about it, Jacob,"

Scrooge observed in a business-like manner, though with humility and deference.

"Slow!" the Ghost repeated.

"Seven years dead," mused Scrooge. "And traveling all the time?"

"The whole time," said the Ghost. "No rest, no peace. Incessant torture of remorse."

"You travel fast?" said Scrooge.

"On the wings of the wind," replied the Ghost.

"You might have got over a great quantity of ground in seven years," said Scrooge.

The Ghost, on hearing this, set up another cry, and clanked his chain so hideously in the dead silence of the night, that the Ward would have been justified in indicting it for a nuisance.

"Oh! captive, bound and double-ironed," cried the phantom, "not to know that ages of incessant labor, by immortal creatures, for this earth, must pass into eternity before the good of which it is susceptible is all developed! Not to know that any Christian spirit working kindly in its little sphere, whatever it may be, will find its mortal life too short for its vast means of usefulness! Not to know that no space of regret can make amends for one life's opportunities misused! Yet such was I! Oh! such was I!"

"But you were always a good man of business, Jacob," faltered Scrooge, who now began to apply this to himself.

"Business!" cried the Ghost, wringing his hands again. "Mankind was my business. The common welfare was my business; charity, mercy, forbearance, and benevolence were all my business. The dealings of my trade were but a drop of water in the comprehensive ocean of my business!"

He held up his chain at arm's-length, as if that were the cause of all his unavailing grief, and flung it heavily upon the ground again.

"At this time of the rolling year," the specter said, "I suffer most. Why did I walk through crowds of fellow-beings with my eyes turned down, and never raise them to that blessed Star which led the Wise Men to a poor abode? Were there no poor homes to which its light would have conducted *me?*"

Scrooge was very much dismayed to hear the specter going on at this rate, and began to quake exceedingly.

"Hear me!" cried the Ghost. "My time is nearly gone."

"I will," said Scrooge. "But don't be hard upon me! Don't be flowery, Jacob! Pray!"

"How it is that I appear before you in a shape that you can see, I may not tell. I have sat invisible beside you many and many a day."

It was not an agreeable idea. Scrooge shivered, and wiped the perspiration from his brow.

"That is no light part of my penance," pursued the Ghost. "I am here to-night to warn you, that you have yet a chance and hope of escaping my fate. A chance and hope of my procuring, Ebenezer."

"You were always a good friend to me," said Scrooge. "Thankee!"

"You will be haunted," resumed the Ghost, "by Three Spirits."

Scrooge's countenance fell almost as low as the Ghost's had done.

"Is that the chance and hope you mentioned, Jacob?" he demanded in a faltering voice.

"It is."

"I—I think I'd rather not," said Scrooge.

"Without their visits," said the Ghost, "you cannot hope to shun the path I tread. Expect the first tomorrow. When the bell tolls One."

"Couldn't I take 'em all at once, and have it over, Jacob?" hinted Scrooge.

"Expect the second on the next night at the same hour. The third, upon the next night when the last stroke of Twelve has ceased to vibrate. Look to see me no more; and look that, for your own sake, you remember what has passed between us!"

When he had said these words, the specter took his wrapper from the table, and bound it round his head, as before. Scrooge knew this, by the smart sound his teeth made when the jaws were brought together by the bandage. He ventured to raise his eyes again, and found his supernatural visitor confronting him in an erect attitude, with his chain wound over and about his arm.

The apparition walked backward from him; and at every step he took, the window raised itself a little, so that when the specter reached it, it was wide open. He beckoned Scrooge to approach, which he did. When they were within two paces of each other, Marley's Ghost held up his hand, warning him to come no nearer. Scrooge stopped.

Not so much in obedience, as in surprise and fear; for on the raising of the hand he became sensible of confused noises in the air; incoherent sounds of lamentation and regret; wailings inexpressibly sorrowful and self-accusatory. The specter, after listening for a moment, joined in the mournful dirge; and floated out upon the bleak, dark night.

Scrooge followed to the window, desperate in his curiosity. He looked out.

The air was filled with phantoms, wandering hither and thither in restless haste, and moaning as they went. Every one of them wore chains like Marley's Ghost; some few (they might be guilty governments) were linked together; none were free. Many had been personally known to Scrooge in their lives. He had been quite familiar with one old ghost, in a white waistcoat, with a monstrous iron safe attached to his ankle, who cried piteously at being unable to assist a wretched woman with an infant, whom he saw below, upon a doorstep. The misery with them all was, clearly, that they sought to interfere, for good, in human matters, and had lost the power forever.

Whether these creatures faded into mist, or mist enshrouded them, he could not tell. But they and their spirit voices faded together; and the night became as it had been when he walked home.

Scrooge closed the window, and examined the door by which the Ghost had entered. It was double-locked, as he had locked it with his own hands, and the bolts were undisturbed. He tried to say "Humbug!" but stopped at the first syllable. And being, from the emotion he had undergone, or the fatigues of the day, or his glimpse of the Invisible World, or the dull conversation of the Ghost, or the lateness of the hour, much in need of repose, went straight to bed, without undressing, and fell asleep on the instant.

STAVE TWO

The First of the Three Spirits

When Scrooge awoke it was so dark, that, looking out of bed, he could scarcely distinguish the transparent winßdow from the opaque walls of his chamber. He was endeavoring to pierce the darkness with his ferret eyes, when the chimes of a neighboring church struck the four quarters. So he listened for the hour.

To his great astonishment the heavy bell went on from six to seven, and from seven to eight, and regularly up to twelve; then stopped. Twelve! It was past two when he went to bed. The clock was wrong. An icicle must have got into the works. Twelve!

He touched the spring of his repeater, to correct this most preposterous clock. Its rapid little pulse beat twelve; and stopped.

"Why, it isn't possible," said Scrooge, "that I can have slept through a whole day and far into another night. It isn't possible that anything has happened to the sun, and this is twelve at noon!"

The idea being an alarming one, he scrambled out of bed, and groped his way to the window. He was obliged to rub the frost off with the sleeve of his dressing-gown before he could see anything; and could see very little then. All he could make out was, that it was still very foggy and extremely cold, and that there was no noise of people running to and fro, and making a great stir, as there unquestionably would have been if night had beaten off bright day, and taken possession of the world. This was a great relief, because "Three days after sight of this First of Exchange pay to Mr. Ebenezer Scrooge or his order," and so forth, would have become a mere United States security if there were no days to count by.

Scrooge went to bed again, and thought, and thought, and thought it over and over, and could make nothing of it. The more he thought, the more perplexed he was; and the more he endeavored not to think, the more he thought.

Marley's Ghost bothered him exceedingly. Every time he resolved within himself, after mature inquiry, that it was all a dream, his mind flew back again, like a strong spring released, to its first position, and presented the same problem to be worked all through, "Was it a dream or not?"

Scrooge lay in this state until the chime had gone three quarters more, when he remembered, on a sudden, that the Ghost had warned him of a visitation when the bell tolled One. He resolved to lie awake until the hour was passed; and, considering that he could no more go to sleep than go to Heaven, this was, perhaps, the wisest resolution in his power.

The quarter was so long, that he was more than once convinced he must have sunk into a doze unconsciously, and missed the clock. At length it broke upon his listening ear.

"Ding, dong!"

"A quarter past," said Scrooge, counting.

"Ding, dong!"

"Half past," said Scrooge.

"Ding, dong!"

"A quarter to it," said Scrooge.

"Ding, dong!"

"The hour itself," said Scrooge triumphantly, "and nothing else!"

He spoke before the hour bell sounded, which it now did with a deep, dull, hollow, melancholy ONE. Lights flashed up in the room upon the instant, and the curtains of his bed were drawn.

The curtains of his bed were drawn aside, I tell you, by a hand. Not the curtains at his feet, nor the curtains at his back, but those to which his face was addressed. The curtains of his bed were drawn aside: and Scrooge, starting up into a half-recumbent attitude, found himself face to face with the unearthly visitor who drew them: as close to it as I am now to you, and I am standing in the spirit at your elbow.

It was a strange figure—like a child; yet not so like a child as like an old man, viewed through some supernatural medium, which gave him the appearance of having receded from the view, and being diminished to a child's proportions. Its hair, which hung about its neck and down its back, was white, as if with age; and yet the face had not a wrinkle in it, and the tenderest bloom was on the skin. The arms were very long and muscular; the hands the same, as if its hold were of uncommon strength. Its legs and feet, most delicately formed, were, like those upper members, bare. It wore a tunic of the purest white; and round its waist was bound a lustrous belt, the sheen of which was beautiful. It held a branch of fresh, green holly in its hand; and, in singular contradiction to that wintry emblem, had its dress trimmed with summer flowers. But the strangest thing about it was, that from the crown of its head there sprung a bright, clear jet of light, by which all this was visible; and which was doubtless the occasion of its using, in its duller moments, a great extinguisher for a cap, which it now held under its arm.

Even this, though, when Scrooge looked at it with increasing steadiness, was *not* its strangest quality. For as its belt sparkled and glittered now in one part and now in another, and what was light one instant at another time was dark, so the figure itself fluctuated in its distinctness; being now a thing with one arm, now with one leg, now with twenty legs, now a pair of legs without a head, now a head without a body; of which dissolving parts no outline would be visible in the dense gloom wherein they melted away. And, in the very wonder of this, it would be itself again, distinct and clear as ever.

"Are you the Spirit, sir, whose coming was foretold to me?" asked Scrooge.

"I am!"

The voice was soft and gentle. Singularly low, as if instead of being so close beside him, it were at a distance.

"Who, and what are you?" Scrooge demanded.

"I am the Ghost of Christmas Past."

"Long Past?" inquired Scrooge, observant of its dwarfish stature.

"No. Your past."

Perhaps Scrooge could not have told anybody why,

if anybody could have asked him, but he had a special desire to see the Spirit in his cap, and begged him to be covered.

"What!" exclaimed the Ghost, "would you so soon put out, with worldly hands, the light I give? Is it not enough that you are one of those whose passions made this cap, and force me through whole trains of years to wear it low upon my brow?"

Scrooge reverently disclaimed all intention to offend or any knowledge of having wilfully "bonneted" the Spirit at any period of his life. He then made bold to inquire what business brought him there.

"Your welfare!" said the Ghost.

Scrooge expressed himself as much obliged, but could not help thinking that a night of unbroken rest would have been more conducive to that end. The Spirit must have heard him thinking, for it said immediately:

"Your reclamation, then. Take heed!"

It put out its strong hand as it spoke, and clasped him gently by the arm.

"Rise, and walk with me!"

It would have been in vain for Scrooge to plead that the weather and the hour were not adapted to pedestrian purposes; that his bed was warm, and the thermometer a long way below freezing; that he was clad but lightly in his slippers, dressing-gown, and nightcap; and that he had a cold upon him at that time. The grasp, though gentle as a woman's hand, was not to be resisted. He rose; but finding that the Spirit made toward the window, clasped its robe in supplication.

"I am a mortal," Scrooge remonstrated, "and liable to fall."

"Bear but a touch of my hand *there*," said the Spirit,

laying it upon his heart, "and you shall be upheld in more than this!"

As the words were spoken, they passed through the wall, and stood upon an open country road, with fields on either hand. The city had entirely vanished. Not a vestige of it was to be seen. The darkness and the mist had vanished with it, for it was a clear, cold, winter day, with snow upon the ground.

"Good Heaven!" said Scrooge, clasping his hands together, as he looked about him. "I was bred in this place. I was a boy here!"

The Spirit gazed upon him mildly. Its gentle touch, though it had been light and instantaneous, appeared still present to the old man's sense of feeling. He was conscious of a thousand odors floating in the air, each one connected with a thousand thoughts, and hopes, and joys, and cares long, long forgotten!

"Your lip is trembling," said the Ghost. "And what is that upon your cheek?"

Scrooge muttered, with an unusual catching in his voice, that it was a pimple, and begged the Ghost to lead him where he would.

"You recollect the way?" inquired the Spirit.

"Remember it!" cried Scrooge with fervor, "I could walk it blindfold."

"Strange to have forgotten it for so many years!" observed the Ghost. "Let us go on."

They walked along the road, Scrooge recognizing every gate, and post, and tree; until a little market-town appeared in the distance, with its bridge, its church, and winding river. Some shaggy ponies now were seen trotting toward them, with boys upon their backs, who called to other boys in country gigs and carts, driven by farmers. All these boys were in great spirits, and shouted to each other, until the broad fields were so full of merry music that the crisp air laughed to hear it.

"These are but shadows of the things that have been," said the Ghost. "They have no consciousness of us."

The jocund travelers came on; and as they came, Scrooge knew and named them every one. Why was he rejoiced beyond all bounds to see them? Why did his cold eye glisten, and his heart leap up as they went past? Why was he filled with gladness when he heard them give each other merry Christmas, as they parted at cross-roads and byways, for their several homes? What was merry Christmas to Scrooge? Out upon merry Christmas! What good had it ever done to him?

"The school is not quite deserted," said the Ghost. "A solitary child, neglected by his friends, is left there still."

Scrooge said he knew it. And he sobbed.

They left the highroad, by a well-remembered lane, and soon approached a mansion of dull red brick, with a little weathercock-surmounted cupola, on the roof, and a bell hanging in it. It was a large house, but one of broken fortunes; for the spacious offices were little used, their walls were damp and mossy, their windows broken, and their gates decayed. Fowls clucked and strutted in the stables, and the coach-houses and sheds were overrun with grass. Nor was it more retentive of its ancient state, within; for entering the dreary hall, and glancing through the open doors of many rooms, they found them poorly furnished, cold, and vast. There was an earthy savor in the air, a chilly bareness in the place, which associated itself somehow with too much getting up by candlelight, and not too much to eat.

They went, the Ghost and Scrooge, across the hall, to a door at the back of the house. It opened before them, and disclosed a long, bare, melancholy room, made barer still by lines of plain deal forms and desks. At one of these a lonely boy was reading near a feeble fire; and Scrooge sat down upon a form, and wept to see his poor forgotten self as he had used to be.

Not a latent echo in the house, not a squeak and scuffle from the mice behind the paneling, not a drip from the half-thawed water-spout in the dull yard behind, not a sigh among the leafless boughs of one despondent poplar, not the idle swinging of an empty storehouse door, no, not a clicking in the fire, but fell upon the heart of Scrooge with softening influence, and gave a freer passage to his tears.

The Spirit touched him on the arm, and pointed to his younger self, intent upon his reading. Suddenly a man, in foreign garments, wonderfully real and distinct to look at, stood outside the window, with an ax stuck in his belt, and leading by the bridle an ass laden with wood.

"Why, it's Ali Baba!" Scrooge exclaimed in ecstasy. "It's dear old honest Ali Baba! Yes, yes, I know! One Christmas-time, when yonder solitary child was left here all alone, he *did* come, for the first time, just like that. Poor boy! And Valentine," said Scrooge, "and his wild brother Orson; there they go! And what's his name, who was put down in his drawers, asleep, at the Gate of Damascus; don't you see him? And the Sultan's Groom turned upside down by the Genii; there he is upon his head! Serve him right! I'm glad of it. What business had *he* to be married to the Princess?"

To hear Scrooge expending all the earnestness of his nature on such subjects, in a most extraordinary voice between laughing and crying, and to see his heightened and excited face, would have been a surprise to his business friends in the City, indeed.

"There's the Parrot!" cried Scrooge. "Green body and yellow tail, with a thing like a lettuce growing out of the top of his head; there he is! Poor Robin Crusoe, he called him, when he came home again, after sailing round the island. 'Poor Robin Crusoe, where have you been, Robin Crusoe?' The man thought he was dreaming, but he wasn't. It was the Parrot, you know. There goes Friday, running for his life to the little creek! Halloa! Hoop! Halloa!"

Then, with a rapidity of transition very foreign to his usual character, he said, in pity for his former self, "Poor boy!" and cried again.

"I wish," Scrooge muttered, putting his hand in his pocket, and looking about him, after drying his eyes with his cuff, "but it's too late now."

"What is the matter?" asked the Spirit.

"Nothing," said Scrooge, "nothing. There was a boy singing a Christmas carol at my door last night. I should like to have given him something, that's all."

The Ghost smiled thoughtfully, and waved its hand, saying, as it did so, "Let us see another Christmas!"

Scrooge's former self grew larger at the words, and the room became a little darker and more dirty. The panels shrunk, the windows cracked; fragments of plaster fell out of the ceiling, and the naked laths were shown instead; but how all this was brought about, Scrooge knew no more than you do. He only knew that it was quite correct; that everything had happened so; that there he was, alone again, when all the other boys had gone home for the jolly holidays.

He was not reading now, but walking up and down

despairingly. Scrooge looked at the Ghost, and, with a mournful shaking of his head, glanced anxiously toward the door.

It opened, and a little girl, much younger than the boy, came darting in, and, putting her arms around his neck, and often kissing him, addressed him as her "dear, dear brother."

"I have come to bring you home, dear brother!" said the child, clapping her tiny hands, and bending down to laugh. "To bring you home, home, home!"

"Home, little Fan?" returned the boy.

"Yes!" said the child, brimful of glee. "Home, for good and all. Home, for ever and ever. Father is so much kinder than he used to be, that home's like Heaven! He spoke so gently to me one dear night when I was going to bed that I was not afraid to ask him once more if you might come home; and he said Yes, you should; and sent me in a coach to bring you. And you're to be a man!" said the child, opening her eyes, "and are never to come back here; but first, we're to be together all the Christmas long, and have the merriest time in all the world."

"You are quite a woman, little Fan!" exclaimed the boy.

She clapped her hands and laughed, and tried to touch his head; but, being too little, laughed again, and stood on tiptoe to embrace him. Then she began to drag him, in her childish eagerness, toward the door; and he, nothing loath to go, accompanied her.

A terrible voice in the hall cried, "Bring down Master Scrooge's box, there!" and in the hall appeared the schoolmaster himself, who glared on Master Scrooge with a ferocious condescension, and threw him into a dreadful state of mind by shaking hands with him.

He then conveyed him and his sister into the veriest old well of a shivering best parlor that ever was seen, where the maps upon the wall, and the celestial and terrestrial globes in the windows, were waxy with cold. Here he produced a decanter of curiously light wine, and a block of curiously heavy cake, and administered instalments of those dainties to the young people; at the same time, sending out a meager servant to offer a glass of "something" to the postboy, who answered that he thanked the gentleman, but if it was the same tap as he had tasted before, he had rather not. Master Scrooge's trunk being by this time tied on to the top of the chaise, the children bade the schoolmaster good-by right willingly; and, getting into it, drove gaily down the garden sweep, the quick wheels dashing the hoar-frost and snow from off the dark leaves of the ever-greens like spray.

"Always a delicate creature, whom a breath might have withered," said the Ghost. "But she had a large heart!"

"So she had," cried Scrooge. "You're right. I will not gainsay it, Spirit. God forbid!"

"She died a woman," said the Ghost, "and had, as I think, children."

"One child," Scrooge returned.

"True," said the Ghost. "Your nephew!"

Scrooge seemed uneasy in his mind and answered briefly, "Yes."

Although they had but that moment left the school behind them, they were now in the busy thorough-fares of a city, where shadowy passengers passed and repassed, where shadowy carts and coaches battled for the way, and all the strife and tumult of a real city were. It was made plain enough, by the dressing of the shops, that here, too, it was Christmas-time again, but it was evening, and the streets were lighted up.

The Ghost stopped at a certain warehouse door, and asked Scrooge if he knew it.

"Know it!" said Scrooge. "Was I apprenticed here!"

They went in. At sight of an old gentleman in a Welsh wig, sitting behind such a high desk that if he had been two inches taller he must have knocked his head against the ceiling, Scrooge cried in great excitement:

"Why, it's old Fezziwig! Bless his heart; it's Fezziwig alive again!"

Old Fezziwig laid down his pen, and looked up at the clock, which pointed to the hour of seven. He rubbed his hands, adjusted his capacious waistcoat, laughed all over himself, from his shoes to his organ of benevolence and called out, in a comfortable, oily, rich, fat, jovial voice:

"Yo ho, there! Ebenezer! Dick!"

Scrooge's former self, now grown a young man, came briskly in, accompanied by his fellow-prentice.

"Dick Wilkins, to be sure!" said Scrooge to the Ghost. "Bless me, yes. There he is. He was very much attached to me, was Dick. Poor Dick! Dear, dear!"

"Yo ho, my boys!" said Fezziwig. "No more work to-night. Christmas Eve, Dick. Christmas, Ebenezer! Let's have the shutters up," cried old Fezziwig, with a sharp clap of his hands, "before a man can say Jack Robinson!"

You wouldn't believe how those two fellows went at it! They charged into the street with the shutters—one, two, three—had 'em up in their places—four, five, six—barred 'em and pinned 'em—seven, eight, nine—and came back before you could have got to twelve, panting like racehorses.

"Hilli-ho!" cried old Fezziwig, skipping down from the high desk with wonderful agility. "Clear away, my lads, and let's have lots of room here! Hilli-ho, Dick! Chirrup, Ebenezer!"

Clear away! There was nothing they wouldn't have cleared away, or couldn't have cleared away, with old Fezziwig looking on. It was done in a minute. Every movable was packed off, as if it were dismissed from public life forevermore; the floor was swept and watered, the lamps were trimmed, fuel was heaped upon the fire; and the warehouse was as snug, and warm, and dry, and bright a ballroom as you would desire to see upon a winter's night.

In came a fiddler with a music-book, and went up to the lofty desk, and made an orchestra of it, and tuned like fifty stomach-aches. In came Mrs. Fezziwig, one vast, substantial smile. In came the three Miss Fezziwigs, beaming and lovable. In came the six young followers whose hearts they broke. In came all the young men and women employed in the business. In came the house-maid, with her cousin, the baker. In came the cook, with her brother's particular friend, the milkman. In came the boy from over the way, who was suspected of not having board enough from his master, trying to hide himself behind the girl from next door but one, who was proved to have had her ears pulled by her mistress. In they all came, one after another; some shyly, some boldly, some gracefully, some awkwardly, some pushing, some pulling; in they all came, anyhow and everyhow. Away they all went, twenty couple at once; hands half round and back again the other way; down the middle and up again; round and round in various stages of affectionate grouping; old top couple always turning up in the wrong place; new top couple starting off again, as soon as they got there; all top couples at last, and not a bottom one to help them! When this result was brought about, old Fezziwig, clapping his hands to stop the dance, cried out, "Well done!" and the fiddler plunged his hot face into a pot of porter, especially provided for that purpose. But, scorning rest, upon his reappearance he instantly began again, though there were no dancers yet, as if the other fiddler had been carried home, exhausted, on a shutter, and he were a brand-new man resolved to beat him out of sight, or perish.

There were more dances, and there were forfeits, and more dances, and there was cake, and there was negus, and there was a great piece of cold roast, and there was a great piece of cold boiled, and there were mince-pies, and plenty of beer. But the great effect of the evening came after the roast and boiled, when the fiddler (an artful dog, mind! the sort of man who knew his business better than you or I could have told it him!) struck up "Sir Roger de Coverley." Then old Fezziwig stood out to dance with Mrs. Fezziwig. Top couple, too, with a good stiff piece of work cut out for them; three or four and twenty pair of partners; people who were not to be trifled with; people who *would* dance, and had no notion of walking.

But if they had been twice as many—ah, four times—old Fezziwig would have been a match for them, and so would Mrs. Fezziwig. As to *her*, she was worthy to be his partner in every sense of the term. If that's not high praise, tell me higher, and I'll use it. A positive light appeared to issue from Fezziwig's calves. They shone in every part of the dance like moons. You couldn't have predicted, at any given time, what would become of them next. And when old Fezziwig and Mrs. Fezziwig had gone all through the dance; advance and retire, both hands to your partner, bow and curtsey, corkscrew, thread-the-needle, and back again to your place, Fezziwig "cut"—cut so deftly, that he appeared to wink with his legs, and came upon his feet again without a stagger.

When the clock struck eleven, this domestic ball broke up. Mr. and Mrs. Fezziwig took their stations, one on either side of the door, and shaking hands with every person individually as he or she went out, wished him or her a merry Christmas. When everybody had retired but the two prentices, they did the same to them; and thus the cheerful voices died away, and the lads were left to their beds, which were under a counter in the back shop.

During the whole of this time, Scrooge had acted like a man out of his wits. His heart and soul were in the scene, and with his former self. He corroborated everything, remembered everything, enjoyed everything, and underwent the strangest agitation. It was not until now, when the bright faces of his former self and Dick were turned from them, that he remembered the Ghost, and became conscious that it was looking full upon him, while the light upon its head burned very clear.

"A small matter," said the Ghost, "to make these silly folks so full of gratitude."

"Small!" echoed Scrooge.

The Spirit signed to him to listen to the two apprentices, who were pouring out their hearts in praise of Fezziwig, and, when he had done so, said:

"Why! Is it not? He has spent but a few pounds of your mortal money: three or four, perhaps. Is that so much that he deserves this praise?"

"It isn't that," said Scrooge, heated by the remark, and speaking unconsciously like his former, not his latter self—"it isn't that, Spirit. He has the power to render us happy or unhappy, to make our service light or burdensome, a pleasure or a toil. Say that his power lies in words and looks, in things so slight and insignificant that it is impossible to add and count 'em up; what then? The happiness he gives is quite as great as if it cost a fortune."

He felt the Spirit's glance, and stopped.

"What is the matter?" asked the Ghost.

"Nothing particular," said Scrooge.

"Something, I think?" the Ghost insisted.

"No," said Scrooge—"no. I should like to be able to say a word or two to my clerk just now. That's all."

His former self turned down the lamps as he gave utterance to the wish; and Scrooge and the Ghost again stood side by side in the open air.

"My time grows short," observed the Spirit. "Quick!"

This was not addressed to Scrooge, or to any one whom he could see, but it produced an immediate effect. For again Scrooge saw himself. He was older now, a man in the prime of life. His face had not the harsh and rigid lines of later years, but it had begun to wear the signs of care and avarice. There was an eager, greedy, restless motion in the eye, which showed the passion that had taken root, and where the shadow of the growing tree would fall.

He was not alone, but sat by the side of a fair young girl in a mourning-dress, in whose eyes there were tears, which sparkled in the light that shone out of the Ghost of Christmas Past.

"It matters little," she said softly. "To you, very little. Another idol has displaced me; and if it can cheer and comfort you in time to come, as I would have tried to do, I have no just cause to grieve."

"What idol has displaced you?" he rejoined.

"A golden one."

"This is the even-handed dealing of the world!" he said. "There is nothing on which it is so hard as poverty; and there is nothing it professes to condemn with such severity as the pursuit of wealth!"

"You fear the world too much," she answered gently. "All your other hopes have merged into the hope of being beyond the chance of its sordid reproach. I have seen your nobler aspirations fall off one by one, until the master passion, Gain, engrosses you. Have I not?"

"What then?" he retorted. "Even if I have grown so much wiser, what then? I am not changed toward you."

She shook her head.

"Am I?"

"Our contract is an old one. It was made when we were both poor, and content to be so, until, in good season, we could improve our worldly fortune by our patient industry. You *are* changed. When it was made, you were another man."

"I was a boy," he said impatiently.

"Your own feeling tells you that you were not what you are," she returned. "I am. That which promised happiness when we were one in heart is fraught with misery now that we are two. How often and how keenly I have thought of this, I will not say. It is enough that I *have* thought of it, and can release you."

"Have I ever sought release?"

"In words? No. Never."

"In what, then?"

"In a changed nature, in an altered spirit, in another atmosphere of life, another Hope as its great end. In everything that made my love of any worth or value in your sight. If this had never been between us," said the girl, looking mildly, but with steadiness, upon him, "tell me, would you seek me out and try to win me now? Ah, no!"

He seemed to yield to the justice of this supposition, in spite of himself. But he said, with a struggle, "You think not."

"I would gladly think otherwise if I could," she answered. "Heaven knows! When I have learned a Truth like this, I know how strong and irresistible it must be. But if you were free to-day, to-morrow, yesterday, can even I believe that you would choose a dowerless girl—you who, in your very confidence with her, weigh everything by Gain; or, choosing her, if for a moment you were false enough to your own guiding principle to do so, do I not know that your repentance and regret would surely follow? I do, and I release you. With a full heart, for the love of him you once were."

He was about to speak, but, with her head turned from him, she resumed:

"You may—the memory of what is past half makes me hope you will—have pain in this. A very, very brief time, and you will dismiss the recollection of it, gladly, as an unprofitable dream, from which it happened well that you awoke. May you be happy in the life you have chosen!"

She left him, and they parted.

"Spirit!" said Scrooge, "show me no more! Conduct me home. Why do you delight to torture me?"

"One shadow more!" exclaimed the Ghost.

"No more!" cried Scrooge—"no more. I don't wish to see it. Show me no more!"

But the relentless Ghost pinioned him in both his arms, and forced him to observe what happened next.

They were in another scene and place, a room, not very large or handsome, but full of comfort. Near to the winter fire sat a beautiful young girl, so like that last that Scrooge believed it was the same, until he saw *her*, now a comely matron, sitting opposite her daughter. The noise in this room was perfectly tumultuous, for there were more children there than Scrooge in his agitated state of mind could count; and, unlike the celebrated herd in the poem, they were not forty children conducting themselves like one, but every child was conducting itself like forty. The consequences were uproarious beyond belief; but no one seemed to care; on the contrary, the mother and daughter laughed heartily, and enjoyed it very much; and the latter, soon beginning to mingle in the sports, got pillaged by the young brigands most ruthlessly. What would I not have given to be one of them! Though I never could have been so rude, no, no! I wouldn't for the wealth of all the world have crushed that braided hair, and torn it down; and for the precious little shoe, I wouldn't have plucked it off, God bless my soul! to save my life. As to measuring her waist in sport, as they did, bold young brood, I couldn't have done it; I should have expected my arm to have grown round it for a punishment, and never come straight again. And yet I should have dearly liked, I own, to have touched her lips; to have questioned her, that she might have opened them; to have looked upon the lashes of her downcast eyes, and never raised a blush; to have let loose waves of hair, an inch of which would be a keepsake beyond price;

in short, I should have liked, I do confess, to have had the lightest license of a child, and yet to have been man enough to know its value.

But now a knocking at the door was heard, and such a rush immediately ensued that she, with laughing face and plundered dress, was borne toward it, in the center of a flushed and boisterous group, just in time to greet the father, who came home attended by a man laden with Christmas toys and presents. Then the shouting and the struggling, and the onslaught that was made on the defenseless porter! The scaling him, with chairs for ladders, to dive into his pockets, despoil him of brown-paper parcels, hold on tight by his cravat, hug him round the neck, pommel his back, and kick his legs in irrepressible affection! The shouts of wonder and delight with which the development of every package was received! The terrible announcement that the baby had been taken in the act of putting a doll's frying-pan into his mouth, and was more than suspected of having swallowed a fictitious turkey, glued on a wooden platter! The immense relief of finding this a false alarm! The joy, and gratitude, and ecstasy! They are all indescribable alike. It is enough that, by degrees, the children and their emotions got out of the parlor, and, by one stair at a time, up to the top of the house, where they went to bed, and so subsided.

And now Scrooge looked on more attentively than ever, when the master of the house, having his daughter leaning fondly on him, sat down with her and her mother at his own fireside; and when he thought that such another creature, quite as graceful and as full of promise, might have called him father, and been a springtime in the haggard winter of his life, his sight grew very dim indeed.

"Belle," said the husband, turning to his wife with a smile, "I saw an old friend of yours this afternoon."

"Who was it?"

"Guess!"

"How can I? Tut, don't I know?" she added in the same breath, laughing as he laughed. "Mr. Scrooge."

"Mr. Scrooge it was. I passed his office window; and as it was not shut up, and he had a candle inside, I could scarcely help seeing him. His partner lies upon the point of death, I hear, and there he sat alone. Quite alone in the world, I do believe."

"Spirit!" said Scrooge, in a broken voice, "remove me from this place."

"I told you these were shadows of the things that have been," said the Ghost. "That they are what they are, do not blame me!"

"Remove me!" Scrooge exclaimed. "I cannot bear it!"

He turned upon the Ghost, and, seeing that it looked upon him with a face in which, in some strange way, there were fragments of all the faces it had shown him, wrestled with it.

"Leave me! Take me back! Haunt me no longer!"

In the struggle, if that can be called a struggle in which the Ghost, with no visible resistance on its own part, was undisturbed by any effort of its adversary, Scrooge observed that its light was burning high and bright, and dimly connecting that with its influence over him, he seized the extinguisher-cap, and by a sudden action pressed it down upon its head.

The Spirit dropped beneath it, so that the extinguisher covered its whole form, but though Scrooge pressed it down with all his force, he could not hide the light, which streamed from under it in an unbroken flood upon the ground.

He was conscious of being exhausted, and overcome by an irresistible drowsiness, and, further, of being in his own bedroom. He gave the cap a parting squeeze, in which his hand relaxed, and had barely time to reel to bed before he sank into a heavy sleep.

STAVE THREE

The Second of the Three Spirits

Awaking in the middle of a prodigiously tough snore, and sitting up in bed to get his thoughts together, Scrooge had no occasion to be told that the bell was again upon the stroke of One. He felt that he was restored to consciousness in the right nick of time, for the especial purpose of holding a conference with the second messenger despatched to him through Jacob Marley's intervention. But, finding that he turned uncomfortably cold when he began to wonder which of his curtains this new specter would draw back, he put them every one aside with his own hands, and, lying down again, established a sharp lookout all around the bed. For he wished to challenge the Spirit on the moment of its appearance, and did not wish to be taken by surprise, and made nervous.

Gentlemen of the free-and-easy sort, who plume themselves on being acquainted with a move or two, and being usually equal to the time of day, express the wide range of their capacity for adventure by observing that they are good for anything from pitch-and-toss to manslaughter; between which opposite extremes, no doubt, there lies a tolerably wide and comprehensive range of subjects. Without venturing for Scrooge quite as hardly as this, I don't mind calling on you to believe that he was ready for a good broad field of strange appearances, and that nothing between a baby and a rhinoceros would have astonished him very much.

Now, being prepared for almost anything, he was not by any means prepared for nothing; and, consequently, when the bell struck One, and no shape appeared, he was taken with a violent fit of trembling. Five minutes, ten minutes, a quarter of an hour went by, yet nothing came. All this time he lay upon his bed, the very core and center of a blaze of ruddy light, which streamed upon it when the clock proclaimed the hour; and which, being only light, was more alarming than a dozen ghosts, as he was powerless to make out what it meant, or would be at; and was sometimes apprehensive that he might be at that very moment an interesting case of spontaneous combustion, without having the consolation of knowing it. At last, however, he began to think—as you or I would have thought at first; for it is always the person not in the predicament who knows what ought to have been done in it, and would unquestionably have done it too—at last, I say, he began to think that the source and secret of this ghostly light might be in the adjoining room, from whence, on further tracing it, it seemed to shine. This idea taking full possession of his mind, he got up softly, and shuffled in his slippers to the door.

The moment Scrooge's hand was on the lock, a strange voice called him by his name, and bade him enter. He obeyed.

It was his own room. There was no doubt about that. But it had undergone a surprising transformation. The walls and ceiling were so hung with living green that it looked a perfect grove; from every part of which bright, gleaming berries glistened. The crisp leaves of holly, mistletoe, and ivy reflected back the light, as if so many little mirrors had been scattered there, and such a mighty blaze went roaring up the chimney, as that dull petrifaction of a hearth had never known in Scrooge's time, or Marley's, or for many a winter season gone. Heaped up on the floor, to form a kind of throne, were turkeys, geese, game, poultry, brawn, great joints of meat, sucking-pigs, long wreaths of sausages, mince-pies, plum-puddings, barrels of oysters, red-hot chestnuts, cherry-cheeked apples, juicy oranges, luscious pears, immense twelfth-cakes, and seething bowls of punch, that made the chamber dim with their delicious steam. In easy state upon this couch, there sat a jolly Giant, glorious to see; who bore a glowing torch, in shape not unlike Plenty's horn, and held it up, high up, to shed its light on Scrooge, as he came peeping round the door.

"Come in!" exclaimed the Ghost—"come in! and know me better, man!"

Scrooge entered timidly, and hung his head before this Spirit. He was not the dogged Scrooge he had been; and though the Spirit's eyes were clear and kind, he did not like to meet them.

"I am the Ghost of Christmas Present," said the Spirit. "Look upon me!"

Scrooge reverently did so. It was clothed in one simple, deep-green robe, or mantle, bordered with white fur. This garment hung so loosely on the figure that its capacious breast was bare, as if disdaining to be warded or concealed by any artifice. Its feet, observable beneath the ample folds of the garment, were also bare, and on its head it wore no other covering than a holly wreath, set here and there with shining icicles. Its dark-brown curls were long and free, free as its genial face, its sparkling eye, its open hand, its cheery voice, its unconstrained demeanor, and its joyful air. Girded round its middle was an antique scabbard, but no sword was in it, and the ancient sheath was eaten up with rust.

"You have never seen the like of me before!" exclaimed the Spirit.

"Never," Scrooge made answer to it.

"Have never walked forth with the younger members of my family, meaning (for I am very young) my elder brothers born in these later years?" pursued the Phantom.

"I don't think I have," said Scrooge. "I am afraid I have not. Have you had many brothers, Spirit?"

"More than eighteen hundred," said the Ghost.

"A tremendous family to provide for," muttered Scrooge.

The Ghost of Christmas Present rose.

"Spirit," said Scrooge submissively, "conduct me where you will. I went forth last night on compulsion, and I learned a lesson which is working now. To-night, if you have aught to teach me, let me profit by it."

"Touch my robe!"

Scrooge did as he was told, and held it fast.

Holly, mistletoe, red berries, ivy, turkeys, geese, game, poultry, brawn, meat, pigs, sausages, oysters, pies, puddings, fruit, and punch, all vanished instantly. So did the room, the fire, the ruddy glow, the hour of the night, and they stood in the city streets on Christmas morning, where (for the weather was severe) the people made a rough, but brisk and not unpleasant kind of music, in scraping the snow from the pavement in front of their dwellings, and from the tops of their houses, whence it was mad delight to the boys to see it come plumping down into the road below, and splitting into artificial little snow-storms.

The house-fronts looked black enough, and the windows blacker, contrasting with the smooth white sheet of snow upon the roofs, and with the dirtier snow upon the ground; which last deposit had been plowed up in deep furrows by the heavy wheels of carts and wagons, furrows that crossed and recrossed each other hundreds of times where the great streets branched off, and made intricate channels, hard to trace, in the thick yellow mud and icy water. The sky was gloomy, and the shortest streets were choked up with a dingy mist, half thawed, half frozen, whose heavier particles descended in a shower of sooty atoms, as if all the chimneys in Great Britain had, by one consent, caught fire, and were blazing away to their dear hearts' content. There was nothing very cheerful in the climate or the town, and yet there was an air of cheerfulness abroad that the clearest summer air and brightest summer sun might have endeavored to diffuse in vain.

For the people who were shoveling away on the housetops were jovial and full of glee, calling out to one another from the parapets, and now and then exchanging a facetious snowball—better-natured missile far than many a wordy jest—laughing heartily if it went right, and not less heartily if it went wrong. The poulterers' shops were still half open, and the fruiterers' were radiant in their glory. There were great, round, potbellied baskets of chestnuts, shaped like the waistcoats of jolly old gentlemen, lolling at the doors, and tumbling out into the street in their apoplectic opulence. There were ruddy, brown-faced, broad-girthed Spanish onions, shining in the fatness of their growth like Spanish friars, and winking from their shelves in wanton slyness at the girls as they went by, and glanced demurely at the hung-up mistletoe. There were pears and apples, clustered high in blooming pyramids; there were bunches of grapes, made, in the shopkeepers' benevolence, to dangle from conspicuous hooks, that people's mouths might water gratis as they passed; there were piles of filberts, mossy and brown, recalling, in their fragrance, ancient walks among the woods, and pleasant shufflings ankle-deep through withered leaves; there were Norfolk biffins, squab and swarthy, setting off the yellow of the oranges and lemons, and, in the great compactness of their juicy persons, urgently entreating and beseeching to be carried home in paper bags and eaten after dinner. The very gold- and silverfish, set forth among these choice fruits in a bowl, though members of a dull and stagnant-blooded race, appeared to know that there was something going on and, to a fish, went gasping round and round their little world in slow and passionless excitement.

The grocers! oh, the grocers! nearly closed, with perhaps two shutters down, or one, but through those gaps such glimpses! It was not alone that the scales descending on the counter made a merry sound, or that the twine and roller parted company so briskly, or that the canisters were rattled up and down like juggling tricks, or even that the blended scents of tea and coffee were so grateful to the nose, or even that the raisins were so plentiful and rare, the almonds so extremely white, the sticks of cinnamon so long and straight, the other spices so delicious, the candied fruits so caked and spotted with molten sugar as to make the coldest lookers-on feel faint, and subsequently bilious. Nor was it that the figs were moist and pulpy, or that the French plums blushed in modest tartness from their highly decorated boxes, or that everything was good to eat and in its Christmas dress; but the customers were all so hurried and so eager in the hopeful promise of the day, that they tumbled up against each other at the door, crashing their wicker baskets wildly, and left their purchases upon the counter, and came running back to fetch them, and committed hundreds of the like mistakes, in the best humor possible; while the grocer and his people were so frank and fresh that the polished hearts with which they fastened their aprons behind might have been their own, worn outside for general inspection, and for Christmas daws to peck at, if they chose.

But soon the steeples called good people all to church and chapel, and away they came, flocking through the streets in their best clothes, and with their gayest faces. And at the same time there emerged from scores of by-streets, lanes, and nameless turnings, innumerable people, carrying their dinners to the bakers' shops. The sight of these poor revelers appeared to interest the Spirit very much, for he stood, with Scrooge beside him, in a baker's doorway, and, taking off the covers as their bearers passed, sprinkled incense on their dinners from his torch. And it was a very uncommon kind of torch, for once or twice when there were angry words between some dinner-carriers who had jostled each other, he shed a few drops of water on them from it, and their good humor was restored directly. For they said, it was a shame to quarrel upon Christmas Day. And so it was! God love it, so it was!

In time the bells ceased, and the bakers were shut up, and yet there was a genial shadowing forth of all these dinners, and the progress of their cooking, in the thawed blotch of wet above each baker's oven, where the pavement smoked as if its stones were cooking too.

"Is there a peculiar flavor in what you sprinkle from your torch?" asked Scrooge.

"There is. My own."

"Would it apply to any kind of dinner on this day?" asked Scrooge.

"To any kindly given. To a poor one most."

"Why to a poor one most?" asked Scrooge.

"Because he needs it most."

"Spirit," said Scrooge, after a moment's thought, "I wonder you, of all the beings in the many worlds about us, should desire to cramp these people's opportunities of innocent enjoyment."

"I!" cried the Spirit.

"You would deprive them of their means of dining every seventh day, often the only day on which they can be said to dine at all," said Scrooge, "wouldn't you?"

"I!" cried the Spirit.

"You seek to close these places on the Seventh Day," said Scrooge. "And it comes to the same thing."

"*I* seek!" exclaimed the Spirit.

"Forgive me if I am wrong. It has been done in your name, or at least in that of your family," said Scrooge.

"There are some upon this earth of yours," returned the Spirit, "who claim to know us, and who do their deeds of passion, pride, ill will, hatred, envy, bigotry, and selfishness in our name, who are as strange to us, and all our kith and kin, as if they had never lived. Remember that, and charge their doings on themselves, not us."

Scrooge promised that he would and they went on, invisible, as they had been before, into the suburbs of the town. It was a remarkable quality of the Ghost (which Scrooge had observed at the baker's), that notwithstanding his gigantic size, he could accommodate himself to any place with ease, and that he stood beneath a low roof quite as gracefully, and like a supernatural creature, as it was possible he could have done in any lofty hall.

And perhaps it was the pleasure the good Spirit had in showing off this power of his, or else it was his own kind, generous, hearty nature, and his sympathy with all poor men, that led him straight to Scrooge's clerk's; for there he went, and took Scrooge with him, holding to his robe; and on the threshold of the door the Spirit smiled, and stopped to bless Bob Cratchit's dwelling with the sprinklings of his torch. Think of that! Bob had but fifteen "Bob" a week himself; he pocketed on Saturdays but fifteen copies of his Christian name; and yet the Ghost of Christmas Present blessed his four-roomed house!

Then up rose Mrs. Cratchit, Cratchit's wife, dressed out but poorly in a twice-turned gown, but brave in ribbons, which are cheap and make a goodly show for sixpence; and she laid the cloth, assisted by Belinda Cratchit, second of her daughters, also brave in ribbons, while Master Peter Cratchit plunged a fork into the saucepan of potatoes, and getting the corners of his monstrous shirt-collar (Bob's private property, conferred upon his son and heir in honor of the day) into his mouth, rejoiced to find himself so gallantly attired, and yearned to show his linen in the fashionable Parks. And now two smaller Cratchits, boy and girl, came tearing in, screaming that outside the baker's they had smelled the goose, and known it for their own; and basking in luxurious thoughts of sage and onion, these young Cratchits danced about the table, and exalted Master Peter Cratchit to the skies, while he (not proud, although his collars nearly choked him) blew the fire, until the slow potatoes, bubbling up, knocked loudly at the saucepan lid to be let out and peeled.

"What has ever got your precious father, then?" said Mrs. Cratchit. "And your brother, Tiny Tim? And Martha warn't as late last Christmas Day by half an hour!"

"Here's Martha, mother," said a girl, appearing as she spoke.

"Here's Martha, mother!" cried the two young Cratchits. "Hurrah! There's *such* a goose, Martha!"

"Why, bless your heart alive, my dear, how late you are!" said Mrs. Cratchit, kissing her a dozen times, and taking off her shawl and bonnet for her with officious zeal.

"We'd a deal of work to finish up last night," replied the girl, "and had to clear away this morning, mother!"

"Well! Never mind so long as you are come," said Mrs. Cratchit. "Sit ye down before the fire, my dear, and have a warm, Lord bless ye!"

"No, no! There's father coming," cried the two young Cratchits, who were everywhere at once. "Hide, Martha, hide!"

So Martha hid herself, and in came little Bob, the father, with at least three feet of comforter, exclusive of the fringe, hanging down before him, and his thread-bare clothes darned up and brushed, to look season-able, and Tiny Tim upon his shoulder. Alas for Tiny Tim, he bore a little crutch, and had his limbs sup-ported by an iron frame!

"Why, where's our Martha?" cried Bob Cratchit, looking round.

"Not coming," said Mrs. Cratchit.

"Not coming!" said Bob, with a sudden declension in his high spirits for he had been Tim's blood-horse all the way from church, and had come home rampant. "Not coming upon Christmas Day!"

Martha didn't like to see him disappointed, if it were only in joke; so she came out prematurely from behind the closet door, and ran into his arms, while the two young Cratchits hustled Tiny Tim, and bore him off into the washhouse, that he might hear the pudding singing in the copper.

"And how did little Tim behave?" asked Mrs. Cratchit, when she had rallied Bob on his credulity, and Bob had hugged his daughter to his heart's content.

"As good as gold," said Bob, "and better. Somehow he gets thoughtful, sitting by himself so much, and thinks the strangest things you ever heard. He told me, coming home, that he hoped the people saw him in the church, because he was a cripple, and it might be pleasant to them to remember, upon Christmas Day, who made lame beggars walk and blind men see."

Bob's voice was tremulous when he told them this, and trembled more when he said that Tiny Tim was growing strong and hearty.

His active little crutch was heard upon the floor, and back came Tiny Tim before another word was spoken, escorted by his brother and sister to his stool beside the fire; and while Bob, turning up his cuffs—as if, poor fellow, they were capable of being made more shabby—compounded some hot mixture in a jug with gin and lemons, and stirred it round and round, and put it on the hob to simmer, Master Peter and the two ubiquitous young Cratchits went to fetch the goose, with which they soon returned in high procession.

Such a bustle ensued that you might have thought a goose the rarest of all birds, a feathered phenomenon, to which a black swan was a matter of course—and in truth it was something very like it in that house. Mrs. Cratchit made the gravy (ready beforehand in a little saucepan) hissing hot, Master Peter mashed the potatoes with incredible vigor, Miss Belinda sweetened up the apple sauce, Martha dusted the hot plates, Bob took Tiny Tim beside him in a tiny corner at the table, the two young Cratchits set chairs for everybody, not forgetting themselves, and, mounting guard upon their posts, crammed spoons into their mouths, lest they should shriek for goose before their turn came to be helped. At last the dishes were set on, and grace was said. It was succeeded by a breathless pause, as Mrs. Cratchit, looking slowly all along the carving-knife, prepared to plunge it in the breast, but when she did, and when the long-expected gush of stuffing issued forth, one murmur of delight arose all round the board, and even Tiny Tim, excited by the two young Cratchits, beat on the table with the handle of his knife, and feebly cried Hurrah!

There never was such a goose. Bob said he didn't believe there ever was such a goose cooked. Its tenderness and flavor, size and cheapness, were the themes of universal admiration. Eked out by apple sauce and mashed potatoes, it was a sufficient dinner for the whole family; indeed, as Mrs. Cratchit said with great delight (surveying one small atom of a bone upon the dish), they hadn't ate it all at last! Yet every one had enough, and the youngest Cratchits in particular were steeped in sage and onion to the eyebrows! But now, the plates being changed by Miss Belinda, Mrs. Cratchit left the room alone—too nervous to bear witness—to take the pudding up, and bring it in.

Suppose it should not be done enough! Suppose it should break in turning out! Suppose somebody should have got over the wall of the back yard, and stolen it, while they were merry with the goose—a supposition at which the two young Cratchits became livid! All sorts of horrors were supposed.

Hallo! A great deal of steam! The pudding was out of the copper. A smell like a washing-day! That was the cloth. A smell like an eating-house and a pastry-cook's next door to each other, with a laundress's next door to that! That was the pudding! In half a minute Mrs. Cratchit entered—flushed, but smiling proudly—with the pudding, like a speckled cannon-ball, so hard and firm, blazing in half of half a quartern of ignited brandy, and bedight with Christmas holly stuck into the top.

Oh, a wonderful pudding! Bob Cratchit said, and calmly, too, that he regarded it as the greatest success achieved by Mrs. Cratchit since their marriage. Mrs. Cratchit said that, now the weight was off her mind, she would confess she had had her doubts about the quantity of flour. Everybody had something to say about it, but nobody said or thought it was at all a small pudding for a large family. It would have been flat heresy to do so. Any Cratchit would have blushed to hint at such a thing.

At last the dinner was all done, the cloth was cleared, the hearth swept, and the fire made up. The compound in the jug being tasted, and considered perfect, apples and oranges were put upon the table, and a shovelful of chestnuts on the fire. Then all the Cratchit family drew round the hearth in what Bob Cratchit called a circle, meaning half a one, and at Bob Cratchit's elbow stood the family display of glass—two tumblers and a custard-cup without a handle.

These held the hot stuff from the jug, however, as well as golden goblets would have done; and Bob served it out with beaming looks, while the chestnuts on the fire sputtered and crackled noisily. Then Bob proposed:

"A merry Christmas to us all, my dears. God bless us!"

Which all the family re-echoed.

"God bless us, every one!" said Tiny Tim, the last of all.

He sat very close to his father's side, upon his little stool. Bob held his withered little hand in his, as if he loved the child, and wished to keep him by his side, and dreaded that he might be taken from him.

"Spirit," said Scrooge, with an interest he had never felt before, "tell me if Tiny Tim will live."

"I see a vacant seat," replied the Ghost, "in the poor chimney-corner, and a crutch without an owner, carefully preserved. If these shadows remain unaltered by the Future, the child will die."

"No, no," said Scrooge. "Oh, no, kind Spirit! say he will be spared."

"If these shadows remain unaltered by the Future, none other of my race," returned the Ghost, "will find him here. What then? If he be like to die, he had better do it, and decrease the surplus population."

Scrooge hung his head to hear his own words quoted by the Spirit, and was overcome with penitence and grief.

"Man," said the Ghost, "if man you be in heart, not adamant, forbear that wicked cant until you have discovered what the surplus is, and where it is. Will you decide what men shall live, what men shall die? It may be that in the sight of Heaven you are more worthless and less fit to live than millions like this poor man's child. O God! to hear the insect on the leaf pronouncing on the too much life among his hungry brothers in the dust!"

Scrooge bent before the Ghost's rebuke, and, trembling, cast his eyes upon the ground. But he raised them speedily, on hearing his own name.

"Mr. Scrooge!" said Bob; "I'll give you Mr. Scrooge, the Founder of the Feast!"

"The Founder of the Feast, indeed!" cried Mrs. Cratchit, reddening. "I wish I had him here. I'd give him a piece of my mind to feast upon, and I hope he'd have a good appetite for it."

"My dear," said Bob, "the children! Christmas Day."

"It should be Christmas Day, I am sure," said she, "on which one drinks to the health of such an odious, stingy, hard, unfeeling man as Mr. Scrooge. You know he is, Robert! Nobody knows it better than you do, poor fellow!"

"My dear," was Bob's mild answer, "Christmas Day."

"I'll drink to his health for your sake, and the Day's," said Mrs. Cratchit, "not for his. Long life to him! A merry Christmas and a happy New Year! He'll be very merry and very happy, I have no doubt!"

The children drank the toast after her. It was the first of their proceedings which had no heartiness in it. Tiny Tim drank it last of all, but he didn't care twopence for it. Scrooge was the Ogre of the family. The mention of his name cast a dark shadow on the party, which was not dispelled for full five minutes.

After it had passed away, they were ten times merrier than before, from the mere relief of Scrooge the Baleful being done with. Bob Cratchit told them how he had a situation in his eye for Master Peter, which would bring in, if obtained, full five and sixpence weekly. The two young Cratchits laughed tremendously at the idea of Peter's being a man of business, and Peter himself looked thoughtfully at the fire from between his collars, as if he were deliberating what particular investments he should favor when he came into the receipt of that bewildering income. Martha, who was a poor apprentice at a milliner's, then told them what kind of work she had to do, and how many hours she worked at a stretch, and how she meant to lie abed to-morrow morning for a good long rest, to-morrow being a holiday she passed at home. Also how she had seen a countess and a lord some days before, and how the lord "was much about as tall as Peter"; at which Peter pulled up his collars so high that you couldn't have seen his head if you had been there. All this time the chestnuts and the jug went round and round, and by and by they had a song, about a lost child traveling in the snow, from Tiny Tim, who had a plaintive little voice, and sang it very well indeed.

There was nothing of high mark in this. They were not a handsome family, they were not well dressed, their shoes were far from being waterproof, their clothes were scanty, and Peter might have known, and very likely did, the inside of a pawnbroker's. But they were happy, grateful, pleased with one another, and contented with the time; and when they faded, and looked happier yet in the bright sprinklings of the Spirit's torch at parting, Scrooge had his eye upon them, and especially on Tiny Tim, until the last.

By this time it was getting dark, and snowing pretty heavily and as Scrooge and the Spirit went along the streets, the brightness of the roaring fires in kitchens, parlors, and all sorts of rooms was wonderful. Here, the flickering of the blaze showed preparations for a cozy dinner, with hot plates baking through and through before the fire, and deep-red curtains, ready to be drawn to shut out cold and darkness. There, all the children of the house were running out into the snow to meet their married sisters, brothers, cousins, uncles, aunts, and be the first to greet them. Here, again, were shadows on the window-blinds of guests assembling, and there a group of handsome girls, all hooded and fur-booted, and all chattering at once, tripped lightly off to some near neighbor's house, where, woe upon the single man who saw them enter—artful witches! well they knew it—in a glow.

But, if you had judged from the numbers of people on their way to friendly gatherings, you might have thought that no one was at home to give them welcome when they got there, instead of every house expecting company, and piling up its fires half-chimney high. Blessings on it, how the Ghost exulted! How it bared its breadth of breast, and opened its capacious palm, and floated on, outpouring, with a generous hand, its bright and harmless mirth on everything within its reach! The very lamplighter, who ran on before, dotting the dusky street with specks of light, and who was dressed to spend the evening somewhere, laughed out loudly as the Spirit passed, though little kenned the lamplighter that he had any company but Christmas!

And now, without a word of warning from the Ghost, they stood upon a bleak and desert moor, where monstrous masses of rude stone were cast about, as though it were the burial-place of giants, and water spread itself wheresoever it listed, or would have done so, but for the frost that held it prisoner, and nothing grew but moss and furze, and coarse, rank grass. Down in the west the setting sun had left a streak of fiery red, which glared upon the desolation for an instant, like a sullen eye, and, frowning lower, lower, lower yet, was lost in the thick gloom of darkest night.

"What place is this?" asked Scrooge.

"A place where miners live, who labor in the bowels of the earth," returned the Spirit. "But they know me. See!"

A light shone from the window of a hut, and swiftly they advanced toward it. Passing through the wall of mud and stone, they found a cheerful company assembled round a glowing fire. An old, old man and woman, with their children and their children's children, and another generation beyond that, all decked out gaily in their holiday attire. The old man, in a voice that seldom rose above the howling of the wind upon the barren waste, was singing them a Christmas song—it had been a very old song when he was a boy—and from time to time they all joined in the chorus. So surely as they raised their voices, the old man got quite blithe and loud, and so surely as they stopped, his vigor sank again.

The Spirit did not tarry here, but bade Scrooge hold his robe, and, passing on above the moor, sped—whither? Not to sea? To sea. To Scrooge's horror, looking back, he saw the last of the land, a frightful range of rocks, behind them and his ears were deafened by the thundering of water, as it rolled, and roared, and raged among the dreadful caverns it had worn, and fiercely tried to undermine the earth.

Built upon a dismal reef of sunken rocks, some league or so from shore, on which the waters chafed and dashed, the wild year through, there stood a solitary lighthouse. Great heaps of seaweed clung to its base, and storm-birds—born of the wind, one might suppose, as seaweed of the water—rose and fell about it, like the waves they skimmed.

But even here, two men who watched the light had made a fire, that through the loophole in the thick stone wall shed out a ray of brightness on the awful sea. Joining their horny hands over the rough table at which they sat, they wished each other Merry Christmas in their can of grog, and one of them, the elder, too, with his face all damaged and scarred with hard weather, as the figurehead of an old ship might be, struck up a sturdy song that was like a gale in itself.

Again the Ghost sped on, above the black and heaving sea—on, on—until, being far away, as he told Scrooge, from any shore, they lighted on a ship. They stood beside the helmsman at the wheel, the lookout in the bow, the officers who had the watch, dark, ghostly figures in their several stations, but every man among them hummed a Christmas tune, or had a Christmas thought, or spoke below his breath to his companion of some bygone Christmas Day, with homeward hopes belonging to it. And every man on board, waking or sleeping, good or bad, had had a kinder word for another on that day than on any day in the year, and had shared to some extent in its festivities, and had remembered those he cared for at a distance, and had known that they delighted to remember him.

It was a great surprise to Scrooge, while listening to the moaning of the wind, and thinking what a solemn thing it was to move on through the lonely darkness over an unknown abyss, whose depths were secrets as profound as death—it was a great surprise to Scrooge, while thus engaged, to hear a hearty laugh. It was a much greater surprise to Scrooge to recognize it as his own nephew's and to find himself in a bright, dry, gleaming room, with the Spirit standing smiling by his side, and looking at that same nephew with approving affability!

"Ha, ha!" laughed Scrooge's nephew. "Ha, ha, ha!"

If you should happen, by any unlikely chance, to know a man more blessed in a laugh than Scrooge's nephew, all I can say is, I should like to know him, too. Introduce him to me, and I'll cultivate his acquaintance.

It is a fair, even-handed, noble adjustment of things, that, while there is infection in disease and sorrow, there is nothing in the world so irresistibly contagious as laughter and good humor. When Scrooge's nephew laughed in this way, holding his sides, rolling his head, and twisting his face into the most extravagant contortions, Scrooge's niece, by marriage, laughed as heartily as he. And their assembled friends, being not a bit behindhand, roared out lustily.

"Ha, ha! Ha, ha, ha, ha!"

"He said that Christmas was a humbug, as I live!" cried Scrooge's nephew. "He believed it, too!"

"More shame for him, Fred!" said Scrooge's niece

indignantly. Bless those women! they never do any thing by halves. They are always in earnest.

She was very pretty; exceedingly pretty. With a dimpled, surprised-looking capital face, a ripe little mouth that seemed made to be kissed—as no doubt it was; all kinds of good little dots about her chin, that melted into one another when she laughed, and the sunniest pair of eyes you ever saw in any little creature's head. Altogether she was what you would have called provoking, you know, but satisfactory, too. Oh, perfectly satisfactory!

"He's a comical old fellow," said Scrooge's nephew, "that's the truth; and not so pleasant as he might be. However, his offenses carry their own punishment, and I have nothing to say against him."

"I'm sure he is very rich, Fred," hinted Scrooge's niece. "At least you always tell *me* so."

"What of that, my dear?" said Scrooge's nephew. "His wealth is of no use to him. He doesn't do any good with it. He doesn't make himself comfortable with it. He hasn't the satisfaction of thinking—ha, ha, ha!—that he is ever going to benefit us with it."

"I have no patience with him," observed Scrooge's niece. Scrooge's niece's sisters, and all the other ladies, expressed the same opinion.

"Oh, I have!" said Scrooge's nephew. "I am sorry for him: I couldn't be angry with him if I tried. Who suffers by his ill whims? Himself, always. Here, he takes it into his head to dislike us, and he won't come and dine with us. What's the consequence? He doesn't lose much of a dinner."

"Indeed, I think he loses a very good dinner," interrupted Scrooge's niece. Everybody else said the same, and they must be allowed to have been competent judges, because they had just had dinner and, with the dessert upon the table, were clustered round the fire, by lamplight.

"Well! I am very glad to hear it," said Scrooge's nephew, "because I haven't any great faith in these young housekeepers. What do *you* say, Topper?"

Topper had clearly got his eye upon one of Scrooge's niece's sisters, for he answered that a bachelor was a wretched outcast, who had no right to express an opinion on the subject. Whereat Scrooge's niece's sister—the plump one with the lace tucker, not the one with the roses—blushed.

"Do go on, Fred," said Scrooge's niece, clapping her hands. "He never finishes what he begins to say! He is such a ridiculous fellow!"

Scrooge's nephew reveled in another laugh, and as it was impossible to keep the infection off, though the plump sister tried hard to do it with aromatic vinegar, his example was unanimously followed.

"I was only going to say," said Scrooge's nephew, "that the consequence of his taking a dislike to us, and not making merry with us, is, as I think, that he loses some pleasant moments, which could do him no harm. I am sure he loses pleasanter companions than he can find in his own thoughts, either in his moldy old office or his dusty chambers. I mean to give him the same chance every year, whether he likes it or not, for I pity him. He may rail at Christmas till he dies, but he can't help thinking better of it—I defy him—if he finds me going there, in good temper, year after year, and saying, 'Uncle Scrooge, how are you?' If it only puts him in the vein to leave his poor clerk fifty pounds, *that's* something, and I think I shook him, yesterday."

It was their turn to laugh now, at the notion of his

shaking Scrooge. But being thoroughly good-natured, and not much caring what they laughed at, so that they laughed at any rate, he encouraged them in their merriment, and passed the bottle, joyously.

After tea, they had some music. For they were a musical family, and knew what they were about, when they sung a glee or catch, I can assure you: especially Topper, who could growl away in the bass like a good one, and never swell the large veins in his forehead, or get red in the face over it. Scrooge's niece played well upon the harp and played, among other tunes, a simple little air (a mere nothing: you might learn to whistle it in two minutes) which had been familiar to the child who fetched Scrooge from the boarding-school, as he had been reminded by the Ghost of Christmas Past. When this strain of music sounded, all the things that Ghost had shown him came upon his mind; he softened more and more and thought that if he could have listened to it often, years ago, he might have cultivated the kindness of life for his own happiness with his own hands, without resorting to the sexton's spade that buried Jacob Marley.

But they didn't devote the whole evening to music. After a while they played at forfeits, for it is good to be children sometimes, and never better than at Christmas, when its mighty Founder was a child himself. Stop! There was first a game at blind-man's buff. Of course there was. And I no more believe Topper was really blind than I believe he had eyes in his boots. My opinion is, that it was a done thing between him and Scrooge's nephew, and that the Ghost of Christmas Present knew it. The way he went after that plump sister in the lace tucker was an outrage on the credulity of human nature. Knocking down the fire-irons, tum-

bling over the chairs, bumping up against the piano,
smothering himself among the curtains; wherever
she went, there went he! He always knew where the
plump sister was. He wouldn't catch anybody else. If
you had fallen up against him (as some of them did)
on purpose, he would have made a feint of endeavoring to seize you, which would have been an affront to
your understanding, and would instantly have sidled
off in the direction of the plump sister. She often cried
out that it wasn't fair, and it really was not. But when,
at last, he caught her; when, in spite of all her silken
rustlings, and her rapid flutterings past him, he got her
into a corner whence there was no escape, then his conduct was the most execrable. For his pretending not to
know her, his pretending that it was necessary to touch
her head-dress, and further to assure himself of her
identity by pressing a certain ring upon her finger, and
a certain chain about her neck, was vile, monstrous!
No doubt she told him her opinion of it, when, another
blind man being in office, they were so very confiden-
tial together, behind the curtains.

Scrooge's niece was not one of the blindman's-buff
party, but was made comfortable with a large chair
and a footstool, in a snug corner, where the Ghost and
Scrooge were close behind her. But she joined in the
forfeits, and loved her love to admiration with all the
letters of the alphabet. Likewise at the game of How,
When, and Where, she was very great, and, to the secret joy of Scrooge's nephew, beat her sisters hollow,
though they were sharp girls, too, as Topper could
have told you. There might have been twenty people
there, young and old, but they all played, and so did
Scrooge; for, wholly forgetting, in the interest he had
in what was going on, that his voice made no sound in

their ears, he sometimes came out with his guess quite loud, and very often guessed right, too; for the sharpest needle, best Whitechapel, warranted not to cut in the eye, was not sharper than Scrooge, blunt as he took it in his head to be.

The Ghost was greatly pleased to find him in this mood, and looked upon him with such favor, that he begged like a boy to be allowed to stay until the guests departed. But this the Spirit said could not be done.

"Here is a new game," said Scrooge. "One half-hour, Spirit, only one!"

It was a game called Yes and No, where Scrooge's nephew had to think of something, and the rest must find out what, he only answering to their questions yes or no, as the case was. The brisk fire of questioning to which he was exposed, elicited from him that he was thinking of an animal, a live animal, rather a disagreeable animal, a savage animal, an animal that growled and grunted sometimes, and talked sometimes, and lived in London, and walked about the streets, and wasn't made a show of, and wasn't led by anybody, and didn't live in a menagerie, and was never killed in a market, and was not a horse, or an ass, or a cow, or a bull, or a tiger, or a dog, or a pig, or a cat, or a bear. At every fresh question that was put to him, this nephew burst into a fresh roar of laughter and was so inexpressibly tickled, that he was obliged to get up off the sofa and stamp. At last the plump sister, falling into a similar state, cried out:

"I have found it out! I know what it is, Fred! I know what it is!"

"What is it?" cried Fred.

"It's your uncle Scro-o-o-o-oge!"

Which it certainly was. Admiration was the univer-

sal sentiment, though some objected that the reply to
"Is it a bear?" ought to have been "Yes," inasmuch as
an answer in the negative was sufficient to have di-
verted their thoughts from Mr. Scrooge, supposing
they had ever had any tendency that way.

"He has given us plenty of merriment, I am sure,"
said Fred, "and it would be ungrateful not to drink
his health. Here is a glass of mulled wine ready to our
hand at the moment and I say, 'Uncle Scrooge!'"

"Well! Uncle Scrooge!" they cried.

"A merry Christmas and a happy New Year to the
old man, whatever he is!" said Scrooge's nephew. "He
wouldn't take it from me, but may he have it, neverthe-
less. Uncle Scrooge!"

Uncle Scrooge had imperceptibly become so gay
and light of heart, that he would have pledged the
unconscious company in return, and thanked them in
an inaudible speech, if the Ghost had given him time.
But the whole scene passed off in the breath of the last
word spoken by his nephew, and he and the Spirit
were again upon their travels.

Much they saw, and far they went, and many homes
they visited, but always with a happy end. The Spirit
stood beside sick-beds, and they were cheerful; on foreign lands, and they were close at home; by struggling
men, and they were patient in their greater hope; by
poverty, and it was rich. In almshouse, hospital, and
jail, in misery's every refuge, where vain man in his
little brief authority had not made fast the door, and
barred the Spirit out, he left his blessing, and taught
Scrooge his precepts.

It was a long night, if it were only a night, but
Scrooge had his doubts of this, because the Christmas
holidays appeared to be condensed into the space of

time they passed together. It was strange, too, that while Scrooge remained unaltered in his outward form, the Ghost grew older, clearly older. Scrooge had observed this change, but never spoke of it, until they left a children's Twelfth Night party, when, looking at the Spirit as they stood together in an open place, he noticed that its hair was gray.

"Are spirits' lives so short?" asked Scrooge.

"My life upon this globe is very brief," replied the Ghost. "It ends to-night."

"To-night!" cried Scrooge.

"To-night at midnight. Hark. The time is drawing near."

The chimes were ringing the three quarters past eleven at that moment.

"Forgive me if I am not justified in what I ask," said Scrooge, looking intently at the Spirit's robe, "but I see something strange, and not belonging to yourself, protruding from your skirts. Is it a foot or a claw?"

"It might be a claw, for the flesh there is upon it," was the Spirit's sorrowful reply. "Look here."

From the foldings of its robe, it brought two children, wretched, abject, frightful, hideous, miserable. They knelt down at his feet, and clung upon the outside of its garment.

"O Man! look here! Look, look, down here!" exclaimed the Ghost.

They were a boy and girl. Yellow, meager, ragged, scowling, wolfish; but prostrate, too, in their humility. Where graceful youth should have filled their features out, and touched them with its freshest tints, a stale and shriveled hand, like that of age, had pinched and twisted them, and pulled them into shreds. Where angels might have sat enthroned, devils lurked, and glared out menacing. No change, no degradation, no perversion of humanity, in any grade, through all the mysteries of wonderful creation, has monsters half so horrible and dread.

Scrooge started back, appalled. Having them shown to him in this way, he tried to say they were fine children, but the words choked themselves, rather than be parties to a lie of such enormous magnitude.

"Spirit! are they yours?" Scrooge could say no more.

"They are Man's," said the Spirit, looking down upon them. "And they cling to me, appealing from their fathers. This boy is Ignorance. This girl is Want. Beware of them both, and all of their degree, but most of all beware this boy; for on his brow I see that written which is Doom, unless the writing be erased. Deny it!" cried the Spirit, stretching out his hand toward the city. "Slander those who tell it ye! Admit it for your factious purposes, and make it worse! And bide the end!"

"Have they no refuge or resource?" cried Scrooge.

"Are there no prisons?" said the Spirit, turning on him for the last time with his own words. "Are there no workhouses?"

The bell struck Twelve.

Scrooge looked about him for the Ghost, and saw it not. As the last stroke ceased to vibrate, he remembered the prediction of old Jacob Marley, and, lifting up his eyes, beheld a solemn Phantom, draped and hooded, coming, like a mist along the ground, toward him.

STAVE FOUR

The Last of the Spirits

*T*he Phantom slowly, gravely, silently, approached. When it came near him, Scrooge bent down upon his knee, for in the very air through which this Spirit moved it seemed to scatter gloom and mystery.

It was shrouded in a deep black garment, which concealed its head, its face, its form, and left nothing of it visible save one outstretched hand. But for this it would have been difficult to detach its figure from the night, and separate it from the darkness by which it was surrounded.

He felt that it was tall and stately when it came beside him, and that its mysterious presence filled him with a solemn dread. He knew no more, for the Spirit neither spoke nor moved.

"I am in the presence of the Ghost of Christmas Yet to Come?" said Scrooge.

The Spirit answered not, but pointed onward with its hand.

"You are about to show me shadows of the things

that have not happened, but will happen in the time before us," Scrooge pursued. "Is that so, Spirit?"

The upper portion of the garment was contracted for an instant in its folds, as if the Spirit had inclined its head. That was the only answer he received.

Although well used to ghostly company by this time, Scrooge feared the silent shape so much that his legs trembled beneath him, and he found that he could hardly stand when he prepared to follow it. The Spirit paused a moment, as if observing his condition, and giving him time to recover.

But Scrooge was all the worse for this. It thrilled him with a vague uncertain horror, to know that, behind the dusky shroud, there were ghostly eyes intently fixed upon him, while he, though he stretched his own to the utmost, could see nothing but a spectral hand and one great heap of black.

"Ghost of the Future!" he exclaimed, "I fear you more than any specter I have seen. But as I know your purpose is to do me good, and as I hope to live to be another man from what I was, I am prepared to bear you company, and do it with a thankful heart. Will you not speak to me?"

It gave him no reply. The hand was pointed straight before them.

"Lead on!" said Scrooge—"lead on! The night is waning fast, and it is precious time to me, I know. Lead on, Spirit!"

The Phantom moved away as it had come toward him. Scrooge followed in the shadow of its dress, which bore him up, he thought, and carried him along.

They scarcely seemed to enter the City, for the City rather seemed to spring up about them, and encompass them of its own act. But there they were, in the heart of it, on 'Change, among the merchants, who hurried up and down, and chinked the money in their pockets, and conversed in groups, and looked at their watches, and trifled thoughtfully with their great gold seals, and so forth, as Scrooge had seen them often.

The Spirit stopped beside one little knot of business men. Observing that the hand was pointed to them, Scrooge advanced to listen to their talk.

"No," said a great fat man with a monstrous chin. "I don't know much about it either way. I only know he's dead."

"When did he die?" inquired another.

"Last night, I believe."

"Why, what was the matter with him?" asked a third, taking a vast quantity of snuff out of a very large snuff-box. "I thought he'd never die."

"God knows," said the first, with a yawn.

"What has he done with his money?" asked a red-faced gentleman with a pendulous excrescence on the end of his nose, that shook like the gills of a turkey-cock.

"I haven't heard," said the man with the large chin, yawning again. "Left it to his company, perhaps. He hasn't left it to *me*. That's all I know."

This pleasantry was received with a general laugh.

"It's likely to be a very cheap funeral," said the same speaker, "for, upon my life, I don't know of anybody to go to it. Suppose we make up a party, and volunteer?"

"I don't mind going if a lunch is provided," observed the gentleman with the excrescence on his nose. "But I must be fed, if I make one."

Another laugh.

"Well, I am the most disinterested among you, after all," said the first speaker, "for I never wear black gloves, and I never eat lunch. But I'll offer to go, if anybody else will. When I come to think of it, I'm not at all sure that I wasn't his most particular friend, for we used to stop and speak whenever we met. By-by!" •

Speakers and listeners strolled away, and mixed with other groups. Scrooge knew the men, and looked toward the Spirit for an explanation.

The Phantom glided on into a street. Its finger pointed to two persons meeting. Scrooge listened again, thinking that the explanation might lie here.

He knew these men, also, perfectly. They were men of business, very wealthy, and of great importance. He had made a point always of standing well in their esteem—in a business point of view, that is, strictly in a business point of view.

"How are you?" said one.

"How are you?" returned the other.

"Well!" said the first. "Old Scratch has got his own at last, hey?"

"So I am told," returned the second. "Cold, isn't it?"

"Seasonable for Christmas-time. You are not a skater, I suppose?"

"No. No. Something else to think of. Good morning!"

Not another word. That was their meeting, their conversation, and their parting.

Scrooge was at first inclined to be surprised that the Spirit should attach importance to conversations apparently so trivial, but feeling assured that they must have some hidden purpose, he set himself to consider what it was likely to be. They could scarcely be supposed to have any bearing on the death of Jacob, his old partner, for that was Past, and this Ghost's province was the Future. Nor could he think of any one immediately connected with himself, to whom he could apply them. But nothing doubting that, to whomsoever they applied, they had some latent moral for his own improvement, he resolved to treasure up every word he heard, and everything he saw, and especially to observe the shadow of himself when it appeared. For he had an expectation that the conduct of his future self would give him the clue he missed, and would render the solution of these riddles easy.

He looked about in that very place for his own image, but another man stood in his accustomed corner, and though the clock pointed to his usual time of day for being there, he saw no likeness of himself among the multitudes that poured in through the Porch. It gave him little surprise, however, for he had been revolving in his mind a change of life, and thought and hoped he saw his newborn resolutions carried out in this.

Quiet and dark, beside him stood the Phantom, with its outstretched hand. When he roused himself from his thoughtful quest, he fancied, from the turn of the hand and its situation in reference to himself, that the Unseen Eyes were looking at him keenly. It made him shudder, and feel very cold.

They left the busy scene, and went into an obscure part of the town, where Scrooge had never penetrated before, although he recognized its situation, and its bad repute. The ways were foul and narrow, the shops and houses wretched, the people half naked, drunken, slipshod, ugly. Alleys and archways, like so many cesspools, disgorged their offenses of smell, and dirt, and life, upon the straggling streets; and the whole quarter reeked with crime, with filth and misery.

Far in this den of infamous resort, there was a low-browed, beetling shop, below a pent-house roof, where iron, old rags, bottles, bones, and greasy offal were bought. Upon the floor within were piled up heaps of rusty keys, nails, chains, hinges, files, scales, weights, and refuse iron of all kinds. Secrets that few would like to scrutinize were bred and hidden in mountains of unseemly rags, masses of corrupted fat, and sepulchers of bones. Sitting in among the wares he dealt in, by a charcoal stove, made of old bricks, was a gray-haired rascal, nearly seventy years of age, who had screened himself from the cold air without by a frowzy curtaining of miscellaneous tatters, hung upon a line, and smoked his pipe in all the luxury of calm retirement.

Scrooge and the Phantom came into the presence of this man, just as a woman with a heavy bundle slunk into the shop. But she had scarcely entered, when another woman, similarly laden, came in too, and she was closely followed by a man in faded black, who was no less startled by the sight of them than they had been upon the recognition of each other. After a short period of blank astonishment, in which the old man with the pipe had joined them, they all three burst into a laugh.

"Let the charwoman alone to be the first!" cried she who had entered first. "Let the laundress alone to be the second, and let the undertaker's man alone to be the third. Look here, old Joe, here's a chance! If we haven't all three met here without meaning it!"

"You couldn't have met in a better place," said old Joe, removing his pipe from his mouth. "Come into the parlor. You were made free of it long ago, you know, and the other two ain't strangers. Stop till I shut the door of the shop. Ah! How it skreeks! There ain't such a rusty bit of metal in the place as its own hinges, I believe, and I'm sure there's no such old bones here as mine. Ha, ha!

We're all suitable to our calling, we're well matched. Come into the parlor. Come into the parlor."

The parlor was the space behind the screen of rags. The old man raked the fire together with an old stair-rod, and having trimmed his smoky lamp (for it was night) with the stem of his pipe, put it in his mouth again.

While he did this, the woman who had already spoken threw her bundle on the floor, and sat down in a flaunting manner on a stool, crossing her elbows on her knees, and looking with a bold defiance at the other two.

"What odds, then? What odds, Mrs. Dilber?" said the woman. "Every person has a right to take care of themselves. *He* always did!"

"That's true, indeed!" said the laundress. "No man more so."

"Why, then, don't stand staring as if you was afraid, woman! Who's the wiser? We're not going to pick holes in each other's coats, I suppose?"

"No, indeed!" said Mrs. Dilber and the man together. "We should hope not."

"Very well, then!" cried the woman. "That's enough. Who's the worse for the loss of a few things like these? Not a dead man, I suppose?"

"No, indeed," said Mrs. Dilber, laughing.

"If he wanted to keep 'em after he was dead, a wicked old screw," pursued the woman, "why wasn't he natural in his lifetime? If he had been, he'd have had somebody to look after him when he was struck with Death, instead of lying gasping out his last there, alone by himself."

"It's the truest word that ever was spoke," said Mrs. Dilber. "It's a judgment on him."

"I wish it was a little heavier judgment," replied the

woman, "and it should have been, you may depend upon it, if I could have laid my hands on anything else. Open that bundle, old Joe, and let me know the value of it. Speak out plain. I'm not afraid to be the first, nor afraid for them to see it. We knew pretty well that we were helping ourselves, before we met here, I believe. It's no sin. Open the bundle, Joe."

But the gallantry of her friends would not allow of this, and the man in faded black, mounting the breach first, produced *his* plunder. It was not extensive. A seal or two, a pencil-case, a pair of sleeve-buttons, and a brooch of no great value, were all. They were severally examined and appraised by old Joe, who chalked the sums he was disposed to give for each upon the wall, and added them up into a total when he found that there was nothing more to come.

"That's your account," said Joe, "and I wouldn't give another sixpence, if I was to be boiled for not doing it. Who's next?"

Mrs. Dilber was next. Sheets and towels, a little wearing-apparel, two old-fashioned silver teaspoons, a pair of sugar-tongs, and a few boots. Her account was stated on the wall in the same manner.

"I always give too much to ladies. It's a weakness of mine, and that's the way I ruin myself," said old Joe. "That's your account. If you asked me for another penny, and made it an open question, I'd repent of being so liberal, and knock off half a crown."

"And now undo *my* bundle, Joe," said the first woman.

Joe went down on his knees for the greater convenience of opening it, and, having unfastened a great many knots, dragged out a large, heavy roll of some dark stuff.

"What do you call this?" said Joe. "Bed-curtains?"

"Ah!" returned the woman, laughing and leaning forward on her crossed arms. "Bed-curtains!"

"You don't mean to say you took 'em down, rings and all, with him lying there?" said Joe.

"Yes, I do," replied the woman. "Why not?"

"You were born to make your fortune," said Joe, "and you'll certainly do it."

"I certainly sha'n't hold my hand, when I can get anything in it by reaching out, for the sake of such a man as he was, I promise you, Joe," returned the woman coolly. "Don't drop that oil upon the blankets now."

"His blankets?" asked Joe.

"Whose else's do you think?" replied the woman. "He isn't likely to take cold without 'em, I dare say."

"I hope he didn't die of anything catching? Eh?" said old Joe, stopping in his work, and looking up.

"Don't be afraid of that," returned the woman. "I ain't so fond of his company that I'd loiter about him for such things, if he did. Ah! You may look through that shirt till your eyes ache; but you won't find a hole in it, nor a threadbare place. It's the best he had, and a fine one too. They'd have wasted it, if it hadn't been for me."

"What do you call wasting of it?" asked old Joe.

"Putting it on him to be buried in, to be sure," replied the woman, with a laugh. "Somebody was fool enough to do it, but I took it off again. If calico ain't good enough for such a purpose, it isn't good enough for anything. It's quite as becoming to the body. He can't look uglier than he did in that one."

Scrooge listened to this dialogue in horror. As they sat grouped about their spoil, in the scanty light afforded by the old man's lamp, he viewed them with a detestation and disgust which could hardly have been greater though they had been obscene demons, marketing the corpse itself.

"Ha, ha!" laughed the same woman, when old Joe, producing a flannel bag with money in it, told out their several gains upon the ground. "This is the end of it, you see! He frightened every one away from him when he was alive, to profit us when he was dead! Ha, ha, ha!"

"Spirit!" said Scrooge, shuddering from head to foot. "I see, I see. The case of this unhappy man might be my own. My life tends that way now. Merciful Heaven, what is this?"

He recoiled in terror, for the scene had changed, and now he almost touched a bed—a bare, uncurtained bed, on which, beneath a ragged sheet, there lay a something covered up, which, though it was dumb, announced itself in awful language.

The room was very dark, too dark to be observed with any accuracy, though Scrooge glanced round it in obedience to a secret impulse, anxious to know what kind of room it was. A pale light, rising in the outer air, fell straight upon the bed, and on it, plundered and bereft, unwatched, unwept, uncared for, was the body of this man.

Scrooge glanced toward the Phantom. Its steady hand was pointed to the head. The cover was so carelessly adjusted that the slightest raising of it, the motion of a finger upon Scrooge's part, would have disclosed the face. He thought of it, felt how easy it would be to do, and longed to do it, but had no more power to withdraw the veil than to dismiss the specter at his side.

Oh cold, cold, rigid, dreadful Death, set up thine altar here, and dress it with such terrors as thou hast at thy command, for this is thy dominion! But of the loved, revered, and honored head, thou canst not turn one hair to thy dread purposes, or make one feature odious. It is not that the hand is heavy, and will fall down when released; it is not that the heart and pulse are still: but that the hand was open, generous, and true, the heart brave, warm, and tender, and the pulse a man's. Strike, Shadow, strike! And see his good deeds springing from the wound, to sow the world with life immortal!

No voice pronounced these words in Scrooge's ears, and yet he heard them when he looked upon the bed. He thought, if this man could be raised up now, what would be his foremost thoughts? Avarice, hard dealing, griping cares? They have brought him to a rich end, truly!

He lay, in the dark, empty house, with not a man, a woman, or a child to say he was kind to me in this or that, and for the memory of one kind word I will be kind to him. A cat was tearing at the door, and there was a sound of gnawing rats beneath the hearthstone. What *they* wanted in the room of death, and why they were so restless and disturbed, Scrooge did not dare to think.

"Spirit!" he said, "this is a fearful place. In leaving it, I shall not leave its lesson, trust me. Let us go!"

Still the Ghost pointed with an unmoved finger to the head.

"I understand you," Scrooge returned, "and I would do it, if I could. But I have not the power, Spirit. I have not the power."

Again it seemed to look upon him.

"If there is any person in the town who feels emotion caused by this man's death," said Scrooge, quite agonized, "show that person to me, Spirit, I beseech you!"

The Phantom spread its dark robe before him for a moment, like a wing and withdrawing it, revealed a room by daylight, where a mother and her children were.

She was expecting some one, and with anxious eagerness: for she walked up and down the room, started at every sound, looked out from the window, glanced at the clock, tried, but in vain, to work with her needle, and could hardly bear the voices of her children in their play.

At length the long-expected knock was heard. She hurried to the door, and met her husband, a man whose face was care-worn and depressed, though he was young. There was a remarkable expression in it now, a kind of serious delight of which he felt ashamed, and which he struggled to repress.

He sat down to the dinner that had been hoarding for him by the fire, and when she asked him faintly what news (which was not until after a long silence), he appeared embarrassed how to answer.

"Is it good," she said, "or bad?"—to help him.

"Bad," he answered.

"We are quite ruined?"

"No. There is hope yet, Caroline."

"If *he* relents," she said, amazed, "there is! Nothing is past hope, if such a miracle has happened."

"He is past relenting," said her husband. "He is dead."

She was a mild and patient creature, if her face spoke truth; but she was thankful in her soul to hear it, and she said so, with clasped hands. She prayed forgiveness the next moment, and was sorry, but the worst was the emotion of her heart.

"What the half-drunken woman whom I told you of last night said to me, when I tried to see him and obtain a week's delay, and what I thought was a mere excuse to avoid me, turns out to have been quite true. He was not only very ill, but dying, then."

"To whom will our debt be transferred?"

"I don't know. But before that time we shall be ready with the money and even though we were not, it would be bad fortune indeed to find so merciless a creditor in his successor. We may sleep to-night with light hearts, Caroline!"

Yes. Soften it as they would, their hearts were lighter. The children's faces, hushed and clustered round to hear what they so little understood, were brighter, and it was a happier house for this man's death! The only emotion that the Ghost could show him, caused by the event, was one of pleasure.

"Let me see some tenderness connected with a death," said Scrooge, "or that dark chamber, Spirit, which we left just now will be forever present to me."

The Ghost conducted him through several streets familiar to his feet and, as they went along, Scrooge looked here and there to find himself, but nowhere was he to be seen. They entered poor Bob Cratchit's house—the dwelling he had visited before—and found the mother and children seated round the fire.

Quiet. Very quiet. The noisy little Cratchits were as still as statues in one corner, and sat looking up at Peter, who had a book before him. The mother and her daughters were engaged in sewing. But surely they were very quiet!

"'And he took a child, and set him in the midst of them.'"

Where had Scrooge heard those words? He had not dreamed them. The boy must have read them out, as he and the Spirit crossed the threshold. Why did he not go on?

The mother laid her work upon the table, and put her hand up to her face.

"The color hurts my eyes," she said.

The color? Ah, poor Tiny Tim!

"They're better now again," said Cratchit's wife. "It makes them weak by candle-light; and I wouldn't show weak eyes to your father when he comes home, for the world. It must be near his time."

"Past it, rather," Peter answered, shutting up his book. "But I think he has walked a little slower than he used, these few last evenings, mother."

They were very quiet again. At last she said, and in a steady, cheerful voice, that only faltered once:

"I have known him walk with—I have known him walk with Tiny Tim upon his shoulder very fast indeed."

"And so have I," cried Peter. "Often."

"And so have I," exclaimed another. So had all.

"But he was very light to carry," she resumed, intent upon her work, "and his father loved him so, that it was no trouble—no trouble. And there is your father at the door!"

She hurried out to meet him, and little Bob in his comforter—he had need of it, poor fellow—came in. His tea was ready for him on the hob, and they all tried who should help him to it most. Then the two young Cratchits got upon his knees, and laid, each child, a little cheek against his face, as if they said, "Don't mind it, father. Don't be grieved!"

Bob was very cheerful with them, and spoke pleasantly to all the family. He looked at the work upon the table, and praised the industry and speed of Mrs. Cratchit and the girls. They would be done long before Sunday, he said.

"Sunday! You went to-day, then, Robert?" said his wife.

"Yes, my dear," returned Bob. "I wish you could have gone. It would have done you good to see how green a place it is. But you'll see it often. I promised him that I would walk there on a Sunday. My little, little child!" cried Bob. "My little child!"

He broke down all at once. He couldn't help it. If he could have helped it, he and his child would have been farther apart, perhaps, than they were.

He left the room, and went up-stairs into the room above, which was lighted cheerfully, and hung with Christmas. There was a chair set close beside the child, and there were signs of some one having been there lately. Poor Bob sat down in it, and when he had thought a little and composed himself, he kissed the little face. He was reconciled to what had happened, and went down again quite happy.

They drew about the fire and talked, the girls and mother working still. Bob told them of the extraordinary kindness of Mr. Scrooge's nephew, whom he had scarcely seen but once, and who, meeting him in the street that day, and seeing that he looked a little—"just a little down, you know," said Bob, inquired what had happened to distress him. "On which," said Bob, "for he is the pleasantest-spoken gentleman you ever heard, I told him. 'I am heartily sorry for it, Mr. Cratchit,' he said, 'and heartily sorry for your good wife.' By the by, how he ever knew *that*, I don't know."

"Knew what, my dear?"

"Why, that you were a good wife," replied Bob.

"Everybody knows that," said Peter.

"Very well observed, my boy!" cried Bob. "I hope they do. 'Heartily sorry,' he said, 'for your good wife. If I can be of service to you in any way,' he said, giving me his card, 'that's where I live. Pray come to me.' Now it wasn't," cried Bob, "for the sake of anything he might be able to do for us, so much as for his kind way, that this was quite delightful. It really seemed as if he had known our Tiny Tim, and felt with us."

"I'm sure he's a good soul!" said Mrs. Cratchit.

"You would be sure of it, my dear," returned Bob, "if you saw and spoke to him. I shouldn't be at all surprised—mark what I say!—if he got Peter a better situation."

"Only hear that, Peter," said Mrs. Cratchit.

"And then," cried one of the girls, "Peter will be keeping company with some one, and setting up for himself."

"Get along with you!" retorted Peter, grinning.

"It's just as likely as not," said Bob, "one of these days, though there's plenty of time for that, my dear. But, however and whenever we part from one another, I am sure we shall none of us forget poor Tiny Tim—shall we?—or this first parting that there was among us?"

"Never, father!" cried they all.

"And I know," said Bob—"I know, my dears, that when we recollect how patient and how mild he was, although he was a little, little child, we shall not quarrel easily among ourselves, and forget poor Tiny Tim in doing it."

"No, never, father!" they all cried again.

"I am very happy," said little Bob—"I am very happy!"

Mrs. Cratchit kissed him, his daughters kissed him, the two young Cratchits kissed him, and Peter and himself shook hands. Spirit of Tiny Tim, thy childish essence was from God!

"Specter," said Scrooge, "something informs me that our parting moment is at hand. I know it, but I know not how. Tell me what man that was whom we saw lying dead."

The Ghost of Christmas Yet to Come conveyed him, as before—though at a different time, he thought; indeed, there seemed no order in these latter visions, save that they were in the Future—into the resorts of business men, but showed him not himself. Indeed, the Spirit did not stay for anything, but went straight on, as to the end just now desired, until besought by Scrooge to tarry for a moment.

"This court," said Scrooge, "through which we hurry now is where my place of occupation is, and has been for a length of time. I see the house. Let me behold what I shall be, in days to come!"

The Spirit stopped; the hand was pointed elsewhere.

"The house is yonder," Scrooge exclaimed. "Why do you point away?"

The inexorable finger underwent no change.

Scrooge hastened to the window of his office, and looked in. It was an office still, but not his. The furniture was not the same, and the figure in the chair was not himself. The Phantom pointed as before.

He joined it once again, and, wondering why and whither he had gone, accompanied it until they reached an iron gate. He paused to look round before entering.

A churchyard. Here, then, the wretched man whose

name he had now to learn lay underneath the ground. It was a worthy place. Walled in by houses, overrun by grass and weeds, the growth of vegetation's death, not life; choked up with too much burying, fat with repleted appetite. A worthy place!

The Spirit stood among the graves, and pointed down to One. He advanced toward it, trembling. The Phantom was exactly as it had been, but he dreaded that he saw new meaning in its solemn shape.

"Before I draw nearer to that stone to which you point," said Scrooge, "answer me one question. Are these the shadows of the things that Will be or are they shadows of the things that May be, only?"

Still the Ghost pointed downward to the grave by which it stood.

"Men's courses will foreshadow certain ends, to which, if persevered in, they must lead," said Scrooge. "But if the courses be departed from, the ends will change. Say it is thus with what you show me!"

The Spirit was immovable as ever.

Scrooge crept toward it, trembling as he went; and following the finger, read upon the stone of the neglected grave his own name, EBENEZER SCROOGE.

"Am I that man who lay upon the bed?" he cried, upon his knees.

The finger pointed from the grave to him, and back again.

"No, Spirit! Oh, no, no!"

The finger still was there.

"Spirit!" he cried, tight clutching at its robe, "hear me! I am not the man I was. I will not be the man I must have been but for this intercourse. Why show me this, if I am past all hope?"

For the first time the hand appeared to shake.

"Good Spirit," he pursued, as down upon the ground he fell before it, "your nature intercedes for me, and pities me. Assure me that I yet may change these shadows you have shown me, by an altered life!"

The kind hand trembled.

"I will honor Christmas in my heart, and try to keep it all the year. I will live in the Past, the Present, and the Future. The Spirits of all Three shall strive within me. I will not shut out the lessons that they teach. Oh, tell me I may sponge away the writing on this stone!"

In his agony he caught the spectral hand. It sought to free itself, but he was strong in his entreaty, and detained it. The Spirit, stronger yet, repulsed him.

Holding up his hands in a last prayer to have his fate reversed, he saw an alteration in the Phantom's hood and dress. It shrunk, collapsed, and dwindled down into a bedpost.

STAVE FIVE

The End of It

Yes! and the bedpost was his own. The bed was his own, the room was his own. Best and happiest of all, the Time before him was his own, to make amends in!

"I will live in the Past, the Present, and the Future!" Scrooge repeated, as he scrambled out of bed. "The Spirits of all Three shall strive within me. O Jacob Marley! Heaven and the Christmas-time be praised for this! I say it on my knees, old Jacob, on my knees!"

He was so fluttered and so glowing with his good intentions, that his broken voice would scarcely answer to his call. He had been sobbing violently in his conflict with the Spirit, and his face was wet with tears.

"They are not torn down," cried Scrooge, folding one of his bed-curtains in his arms—"they are not torn down, rings and all. They are here—I am here—the shadows of the things that would have been may be dispelled. They will be. I know they will!"

His hands were busy with his garments all this time;

turning them inside out, putting them on upside down, tearing them, mislaying them, making them parties to every kind of extravagance.

"I don't know what to do!" cried Scrooge, laughing and crying in the same breath, and making a perfect Laocoön of himself with his stockings. "I am as light as a feather, I am as happy as an angel, I am as merry as a schoolboy. I am as giddy as a drunken man. A merry Christmas to everybody! A happy New Year to all the world! Hallo here! Whoop! Hallo!"

He had frisked into the sitting-room, and was now standing there, perfectly winded.

"There's the saucepan that the gruel was in!" cried Scrooge, starting off again, and going round the fireplace. "There's the door by which the Ghost of Jacob Marley entered! There's the corner where the Ghost of Christmas Present sat! There's the window where I saw the wandering Spirits! It's all right, it's all true, it all happened. Ha, ha, ha!"

Really, for a man who had been out of practice for so many years, it was a splendid laugh, a most illustrious laugh. The father of a long, long line of brilliant laughs!

"I don't know what day of the month it is," said Scrooge. "I don't know how long I have been among the Spirits. I don't know anything. I'm quite a baby. Never mind. I don't care. I'd rather be a baby. Hallo! Whoop! Hallo here!"

He was checked in his transports by the churches ringing out the lustiest peals he had ever heard. Clash, clash, hammer; ding, dong, bell! Bell, dong, ding; hammer, clang, clash! Oh, glorious, glorious!

Running to the window, he opened it, and put out his head. No fog, no mist; clear, bright, jovial, stirring, cold; cold, piping for the blood to dance to; golden sunlight; heavenly sky; sweet fresh air; merry bells. Oh, glorious! Glorious!

"What's to-day?" cried Scrooge, calling downward to a boy in Sunday clothes, who perhaps had loitered in to look about him.

"Eh?" returned the boy, with all his might of wonder.

"What's to-day, my fine fellow?" said Scrooge.

"To-day!" replied the boy. "Why, *Christmas Day.*"

"It's Christmas Day!" said Scrooge to himself. "I haven't missed it. The Spirits have done it all in one night. They can do anything they like. Of course they can. Of course they can. Hallo, my fine fellow!"

"Hallo!" returned the boy.

"Do you know the poulterer's, in the next street but one, at the corner?" Scrooge inquired.

"I should hope I did," replied the lad.

"An intelligent boy!" said Scrooge. "A remarkable boy! Do you know whether they've sold the prize Turkey that was hanging up there?—Not the little prize Turkey, the big one?"

"What, the one as big as me?" returned the boy.

"What a delightful boy!" said Scrooge. "It's a pleasure to talk to him. Yes, my buck!"

"It's hanging there now," replied the boy.

"Is it?" said Scrooge. "Go and buy it."

"Walk-ER!" exclaimed the boy.

"No, no," said Scrooge. "I am in earnest. Go and buy it, and tell 'em to bring it here, that I may give them the directions where to take it. Come back with the man, and I'll give you a shilling. Come back with him in less than five minutes, and I'll give you half a crown!"

The boy was off like a shot. He must have had a

steady hand at a trigger who could have got a shot off half so fast.

"I'll send it to Bob Cratchit's," whispered Scrooge, rubbing his hands, and splitting with a laugh. "He sha'n't know who sends it. It's twice the size of Tiny Tim. Joe Miller never made such a joke as sending it to Bob's will be!"

The hand in which he wrote the address was not a steady one, but write it he did, somehow, and went down-stairs to open the street door, ready for the coming of the poulterer's man. As he stood there, waiting his arrival, the knocker caught his eye.

"I shall love it as long as I live!" cried Scrooge, patting it with his hand. "I scarcely ever looked at it before. What an honest expression it has in its face! It's a wonderful knocker!—Here's the Turkey. Hallo! Whoop! How are you? Merry Christmas!"

It *was* a Turkey! He never could have stood upon his legs, that bird. He would have snapped 'em short off in a minute, like sticks of sealing-wax.

"Why, it's impossible to carry that to Camden Town," said Scrooge. "You must have a cab."

The chuckle with which he said this, and the chuckle with which he paid for the Turkey, and the chuckle with which he paid for the cab, and the chuckle with which he recompensed the boy, were only to be exceeded by the chuckle with which he sat down breathless in his chair again, and chuckled till he cried.

Shaving was not an easy task, for his hand continued to shake very much and shaving requires attention, even when you don't dance while you are at it. But if he had cut the end of his nose off, he would have put a piece of sticking-plaster over it, and been quite satisfied.

He dressed himself "all in his best," and at last got out into the streets. The people were by this time pouring forth, as he had seen them with the Ghost of Christmas Present; and walking with his hands behind him, Scrooge regarded every one with a delighted smile. He looked so irresistibly pleasant, in a word, that three or four good-humored fellows said, "Good morning, sir! A merry Christmas to you!" And Scrooge said often afterward, that of all the blithe sounds he had ever heard, those were the blithest in his ears.

He had not gone far, when, coming on toward him he beheld the portly gentleman who had walked into his counting-house the day before, and said, "Scrooge and Marley's, I believe?" It sent a pang across his heart to think how this old gentleman would look upon him when they met, but he knew what path lay straight before him, and he took it.

"My dear sir," said Scrooge, quickening his pace, and taking the old gentleman by both his hands, "how do you do? I hope you succeeded yesterday. It was very kind of you. A merry Christmas to you, sir!"

"Mr. Scrooge?"

"Yes," said Scrooge. "That is my name, and I fear it may not be pleasant to you. Allow me to ask your pardon. And will you have the goodness—" Here Scrooge whispered in his ear.

"Lord bless me!" cried the gentleman, as if his breath were taken away. "My dear Mr. Scrooge, are you serious?"

"If you please," said Scrooge. "Not a farthing less. A great many back payments are included in it, I assure you. Will you do me that favor?"

"My dear sir," said the other, shaking hands with him, "I don't know what to say to such munifi—"

"Don't say anything, please," retorted Scrooge. "Come and see me. Will you come and see me?"

"I will!" cried the old gentleman. And it was clear he meant to do it.

"Thankee," said Scrooge. "I am much obliged to you. I thank you fifty times. Bless you!"

He went to church, and walked about the streets, and watched the people hurrying to and fro, and patted the children on the head, and questioned beggars, and looked down into the kitchens of houses, and up to the windows, and found that everything could yield him pleasure. He had never dreamed that any walk—that anything—could give him so much happiness. In the afternoon, he turned his steps toward his nephew's house.

He passed the door a dozen times before he had the courage to go up and knock. But he made a dash, and did it.

"Is your master at home, my dear?" said Scrooge to the girl. Nice girl! Very.

"Yes, sir."

"Where is he, my love?" said Scrooge.

"He's in the dining-room, sir, along with mistress. I'll show you up-stairs, if you please."

"Thankee. He knows me," said Scrooge, with his hand already on the dining-room lock. "I'll go in here, my dear."

He turned it gently, and sidled his face in, round the door. They were looking at the table (which was spread out in great array); for these young housekeepers are always nervous on such points, and like to see that everything is right.

"Fred!" said Scrooge.

Dear heart alive, how his niece by marriage started!

Scrooge had forgotten, for the moment, about her sitting in the corner with the footstool, or he wouldn't have done it, on any account.

"Why, bless my soul!" cried Fred, "who's that?"

"It's I. Your uncle Scrooge. I have come to dinner. Will you let me in, Fred?"

Let him in! It is a mercy he didn't shake his arm off. He was at home in five minutes. Nothing could be heartier. His niece looked just the same. So did Topper, when *he* came. So did the plump sister, when *she* came. So did every one, when *they* came. Wonderful party, wonderful games, wonderful unanimity, won-der-ful happiness!

But he was early at the office next morning. Oh, he was early there! If he could only be there first, and catch Bob Cratchit coming late! That was the thing he had set his heart upon.

And he did it; yes, he did! The clock struck nine. No Bob. A quarter past. No Bob. He was full eighteen minutes and a half behind his time. Scrooge sat with his door wide open, that he might see him come into the tank.

His hat was off before he opened the door; his comforter, too. He was on his stool in a jiffy, driving away with his pen, as if he were trying to overtake nine o'clock.

"Hallo!" growled Scrooge, in his accustomed voice as near as he could feign it. "What do you mean by coming here at this time of day?"

"I am very sorry, sir," said Bob. "I *am* behind my time."

"You are?" repeated Scrooge. "Yes. I think you are. Step this way, sir, if you please."

"It's only once a year, sir," pleaded Bob, appearing

from the tank. "It shall not be repeated. I was making rather merry yesterday, sir."

"Now, I'll tell you what, my friend," said Scrooge, "I am not going to stand this sort of thing any longer. And therefore," he continued, leaping from his stool, and giving Bob such a dig in the waistcoat that he staggered back into the tank again—"and therefore, I am about to raise your salary!"

Bob trembled, and got a little nearer to the ruler. He had a momentary idea of knocking Scrooge down with it, holding him, and calling to the people in the court for help and a strait-waistcoat.

"A merry Christmas, Bob!" said Scrooge, with an earnestness that could not be mistaken, as he clapped him on the back. "A merrier Christmas, Bob, my good fellow, than I have given you for many a year! I'll raise your salary, and endeavor to assist your struggling family, and we will discuss your affairs this very afternoon, over a Christmas bowl of smoking bishop, Bob! Make up the fires, and buy another coal-scuttle before you dot another *i*, Bob Cratchit!"

Scrooge was better than his word. He did it all, and infinitely more; and to Tiny Tim, who did NOT die, he was a second father. He became as good a friend, as good a master, and as good a man as the good old City knew, or any other good old city, town, or borough in the good old world. Some people laughed to see the alteration in him, but he let them laugh, and little heeded them, for he was wise enough to know that nothing ever happened on this globe, for good, at which some people did not have their fill of laughter in the outset; and knowing that such as these would be blind anyway, he thought it quite as well that they should wrinkle up their eyes in grins, as have the malady in less attractive forms. His own heart laughed, and that was quite enough for him.

He had no further intercourse with Spirits, but lived upon the Total Abstinence Principle ever afterward; and it was always said of him, that he knew how to keep Christmas well, if any man alive possessed the knowledge. May that be truly said of us, and all of us! And so, as Tiny Tim observed, God bless Us, Every One!

A
Christmas Tree

(from *Reprinted Pieces*)

❅ ❅ ❅ ❅ ❅ ❅ ❅ ❅ ❅ ❅ ❅ ❅ ❅ ❅ ❅

I have been looking on, this evening, at a merry company of children assembled round that pretty German toy, a Christmas Tree. The tree was planted in the middle of a great round table, and towered high above their heads. It was brilliantly lighted by a multitude of little tapers; and everywhere sparkled and glittered with bright objects. There were rosy-cheeked dolls, hiding behind the green leaves; there were real watches (with movable hands, at least, and an endless capacity of being wound up) dangling from innumerable twigs; there were French-polished tables, chairs, bedsteads, wardrobes, eight-day clocks, and various other articles of domestic furniture (wonderfully made, in tin, at Wolverhampton), perched among the boughs, as if in preparation for some fairy housekeeping; there were jolly, broad-faced little men, much more agreeable in appearance than many real men—and no wonder, for their heads took off, and showed them to be full of sugar-plums; there were fiddles and drums; there were tambourines, books, work-boxes, paint-boxes, sweetmeat-boxes, peep-show boxes, all kinds of boxes; there were trinkets for the elder girls, far brighter than any grown-up gold and jewels; there were baskets and pincushions in all devices; there were guns, swords, and banners; there were witches standing in enchanted rings of pasteboard, to tell fortunes; there were teetotums, humming-tops, needle-cases, pen-wipers, smelling-bottles, conversation-cards, bouquet-holders; real fruit, made artificially dazzling with gold leaf; imitation apples, pears, and walnuts, crammed with surprises; in short, as a pretty child, before me, delightedly whispered to another pretty child, her bosom friend, "There was everything, and more." This motley collection of odd objects clustering on the tree like magic fruit, and flashing back the bright looks directed towards it from every side—some of the diamond-eyes admiring it were hardly on a level with the table, and a few were languishing in timid wonder on the bosoms of pretty mothers, aunts, and nurses—made a lively realisation of the fancies of childhood; and set me thinking how all the trees that grow, and all the things that come into existence on the earth, have their wild adornments at that well-remembered time.

Being now at home again, and alone, the only person in the house awake, my thoughts are drawn back, by a fascination which I do not care to resist, to my own childhood. I begin to consider what do we all remember best upon the branches of the Christmas Tree of our own young Christmas days, by which we climbed to real life.

Straight, in the middle of the room, cramped in the freedom of its growth by no encircling walls or soon-reached ceiling, a shadowy tree arises; and, looking up into the dreamy brightness of its top—for I observe in this tree the singular property that it appears to grow downward towards the earth—I look into my youngest Christmas recollections!

All toys at first, I find. Up yonder, among the green holly and red berries, is the Tumbler, with his hands in his pockets, who wouldn't lie down, but whenever he was put upon the floor, persisted in rolling his fat body about, until he rolled himself still, and brought those lobster eyes of his to bear upon me—when I affected to laugh very much, but in my heart of hearts was extremely doubtful of him. Close beside him is that infernal snuff-box, out of which there sprang a demoniacal Counsellor in a black gown, with an obnoxious head of hair, and a red cloth mouth, wide open, who was not to be endured on any terms, but could not be put away either; for he used suddenly, in a highly magnified state, to fly out of Mammoth Snuff-boxes in dreams, when least expected. Nor is the frog with cobbler's wax on his tail, far off; for there was no knowing where he wouldn't jump; and when he flew over the candle, and came upon one's hand with that spotted back—red on a green ground—he was horrible. The cardboard lady in a blue-silk skirt, who was stood up against the candlestick to dance, and whom I see on the same branch, was milder, and was beautiful; but I can't say as much for the larger cardboard man, who used to be hung against the wall and pulled by a string; there was a sinister expression in that nose of his; and when he got his legs round his neck (which he very often did), he was ghastly, and not a creature to be alone with.

When did that dreadful Mask first look at me? Who put it on, and why was I so frightened that the sight of it is an era in my life? It is not a hideous visage in itself; it is even meant to be a droll; why then were its stolid features so intolerable? Surely not because it hid the wearer's face. An apron would have done as much; and though I should have preferred even the apron away, it would not have been absolutely insupportable, like the mask. Was it the immovability of the mask? The doll's face was immovable, but I was not afraid of *her*. Perhaps that fixed and set change coming over a real face, infused into my quickened heart some remote suggestion and dread of the universal change that is to come on every face, and make it still? Nothing reconciled me to it. No drummers, from whom proceeded a melancholy chirping on the turning of a handle; no regiment of soldiers, with a mute band, taken out of a box, and fitted, one by one, upon a stiff and lazy little set of lazy-tongs; no old woman, made of wires and a brown-paper composition, cutting up a pie for two small children; could give me a permanent comfort, for a long time. Nor was it any satisfaction to be shown the Mask, and see that it was made of paper, or to have it locked up and be assured that no one wore it. The mere recollection of that fixed face, the mere knowledge of its existence anywhere, was sufficient to wake me in the night all perspiration and horror, with, "Oh, I know it's coming! Oh, the mask!"

I never wondered what the dear old donkey with the panniers—there he is!—was made of then! His hide was real to the touch, I recollect. And the great black horse with the round red spots all over him—the horse that I could even get upon—I never wondered what had brought him to that strange condition, or thought that such a horse was not commonly seen at Newmarket. The four horses of no colour, next to him, that went into the wagon of cheeses, and could be taken out and stabled under the piano, appear to have bits of fur-tippet for their tails, and other bits for their manes, and to stand on pegs instead of legs, but it was not so when they were brought home for a Christmas present. They were all right, then; neither was their harness unceremoniously nailed into their chests, as appears to be the case now. The tinkling works of the music-cart, I *did* find out, to be made of quill toothpicks and wire; and I always thought that little tumbler in his shirt sleeves, perpetually swarming up one side of a wooden frame, and coming down, head foremost, on the other, rather a weak-minded person—though good-natured; but the Jacob's Ladder, next him, made of little squares of red wood, that went flapping and clattering over one another, each developing a different picture, and the whole enlivened by small bells, was a mighty marvel and a great delight.

Ah! The Doll's house!—of which I was not proprietor, but where I visited. I don't admire the Houses of Parliament half so much as that stone-fronted mansion with real glass windows, and door-steps, and a real balcony—greener than I ever see now, except at watering-places; and even they afford but a poor imitation. And though it *did* open all at once, the entire house-front (which was a blow, I admit, as cancelling the fiction of a staircase), it was but to shut it up again, and I could believe. Even open, there were three distinct rooms in it: a sitting-room and bedroom, elegantly furnished, and, best of all, a kitchen, with uncommonly soft fire-irons, a plentiful assortment of diminutive utensils—oh, the warming-pan!—and a tin man-cook in profile, who was always going to fry two fish. What Barmecide justice have I done to the noble feasts wherein the set of wooden platters figured, each with its own peculiar delicacy, as a ham or turkey, glued tight on to it, and garnished with something green, which I recollect as moss! Could all the Temperance Societies of these later days, united, give me such a tea-drinking as I have had through the means of yonder little set of blue crockery, which really would hold liquid (it ran out of the small wooden cask, I recollect, and tasted of matches), and which made tea, nectar. And if the two legs of the ineffectual little sugar-tongs did tumble over one another, and want purpose, like Punch's hands, what does it matter? And if I did once shriek out, as a poisoned child, and strike the fashionable company with consternation, by reason of having drunk a little teaspoon, inadvertently dissolved in hot tea, I was never the worse for it, except by a powder!

Upon the next branches of the tree, lower down, hard by the green roller and miniature gardening-tools, how thick the books begin to hang. Thin books, in themselves, at first, but many of them, and with deliciously smooth covers of bright red or green. What fat black letters to begin with! "A was an archer, and shot at a frog." Of course he was. He was an apple pie also, and there he is! He was a good many things in his time, was A, and so were most of his friends, except X, who had so little versatility, that I never knew him to get beyond Xerxes or Xantippe—like Y, who was always confined to a Yacht or a Yew Tree; and Z condemned forever to be a Zebra or a Zany. But, now, the very tree itself changes, and becomes a bean-stalk—the marvellous bean-stalk up which Jack climbed to the Giant's house! And now, those dreadfully interesting, double-headed giants, with their clubs over their shoulders, begin to stride along the boughs in a perfect throng, dragging knights and ladies home for dinner by the hair of their heads. And Jack—how noble, with his sword of sharpness, and his shoes of swiftness! Again those old meditations come back upon me as I gaze up at him; and I debate within myself whether there was more than one Jack (which I am loth to believe possible), or only one genuine original admirable Jack, who achieved all the recorded exploits.

Good for Christmas time is the ruddy colour of the cloak, in which—the tree making a forest of itself for her to trip through, with her basket—Little Red Riding-Hood comes to me one Christmas Eve to give me information of the cruelty and treachery of that dissembling wolf who ate her grandmother, without making any impression on his appetite, and then ate her, after making that ferocious joke about his teeth. She was my first love. I felt that if I could have married Little Red Riding-Hood, I should have known perfect bliss. But it was not to be; and there was nothing for it but to look out the Wolf in the Noah's Ark there, and put him late in the procession on the table, as a monster who was to be degraded. Oh, the wonderful Noah's Ark! It was not found seaworthy when put in a washing-tub, and the animals were crammed in at the roof, and needed to have their legs well shaken down before they could be got in, even there—and then, ten to one, but they began to tumble out the door, which was but imperfectly fastened with a wire latch—but what was *that* against it? Consider the noble fly, a size or two smaller than the elephant: the lady-bird, the butterfly—all triumphs of art! Consider the goose, whose feet were so small, and whose balance was so indifferent, that he usually tumbled forward, and knocked down all the animal creation. Consider Noah and his family, like idiotic tobacco-stoppers; and how the leopard stuck to warm little fingers; and how the tails of the larger animals used gradually to resolve themselves into frayed bits of string!

Hush! Again a forest, and somebody up in a tree—not Robin Hood, not Valentine, not the Yellow Dwarf (I have passed him and all Mother Bunch's wonders, without mention), but an Eastern King with a glittering scimitar and turban. By Allah! two Eastern Kings, for I see another looking over his shoulder! Down upon the grass, at the tree's foot, lies the full length of a coal-black Giant, stretched asleep, with his head in a lady's lap; and near them is a glass box, fastened with four locks of shining steel, in which he keeps the lady prisoner when he is awake. I see the four keys at his girdle now. The lady makes signs to the two kings in the tree, who softly descend. It is the setting-in of the bright Arabian Nights.

Oh, now all common things become uncommon and enchanted to me! All lamps are wonderful, all rings are talismans. Common flower-pots are full of treasure, with a little earth scattered on the top; trees are for Ali Baba to hide in; beefsteaks are to throw down into the Valley of Diamonds, that the precious stones may stick to them, and be carried by the eagles to their nests, whence the traders, with loud cries, will scare them. Tarts are made, according to the recipe of the Vizier's son of Bussorah, who turned pastry-cook after he was set down in his drawers at the gate of Damascus; cobblers are all Mustaphas, and in the habit of sewing up people cut into four pieces, to whom they are taken blindfold.

Any iron ring let into stone is the entrance to a cave which only waits for the magician, and the little fire, and the necromancy, that will make the earth shake. All the dates imported come from the same tree as that unlucky date with whose shell the merchant knocked out the eye of the genie's invisible son. All olives are of the stock of that fresh fruit, concerning which the Commander of the Faithful overheard the boy conduct the fictitious trial of the fraudulent olive merchant; all apples are akin to the apple purchased (with two others) from the Sultan's gardener for three sequins, and which the tall black slave stole from the child. All dogs are associated with the dog, really a transformed man, who jumped upon the baker's counter, and put his paw on the piece of bad money. All rice recalls the rice which the awful lady, who was a ghoule, could only peck by grains, because of her nightly feasts in the burial-place. My very rocking-horse—there he is, with his nostrils turned completely inside-out, indicative of Blood!—should have a peg in his neck, by virtue thereof to fly away with me, as the wooden horse did with the Prince of Persia, in the sight of all his father's Court.

Yes, on every object that I recognise among those upper branches of my Christmas Tree, I see this fairy light! When I wake in bed, at daybreak, on the cold, dark winter mornings, the white snow dimly beheld, outside, through the frost on the window-pane, I hear Dinarzade. "Sister, sister, if you are yet awake, I pray you finish the history of the Young King of the Black Islands." Scheherazade replies, "If my lord the Sultan will suffer me to live another day, sister, I will not only finish that, but tell you a more wonderful story yet." Then the gracious Sultan goes out, giving no orders for the execution, and we all three breathe again.

At this height of my tree I begin to see, cowering among the leaves—it may be born of turkey, or of pudding, or mince-pie, or of these many fancies, jumbled with Robinson Crusoe on his desert island, Philip Quarll among the monkeys, Sanford and Merton with

Mr. Barlow, Mother Bunch, and the Mask—or it may be the result of indigestion, assisted by imagination and over-doctoring—a prodigious nightmare. It is so exceedingly indistinct that I don't know why it's frightful—but I know it is. I can only make out that it is an immense array of shapeless things, which appear to be planted on a vast exaggeration of the lazy-tongs that used to bear the toy soldiers, and to be slowly coming close to my eyes, and receding to an immeasurable distance. When it comes closest, it is worst. In connection with it I descry remembrances of winter nights incredibly long; of being sent early to bed, as a punishment for some small offence, and waking in two hours, with a sensation of having been asleep two nights; of the laden hopelessness of morning ever dawning; and the oppression of a weight of remorse.

And now, I see a wonderful row of little lights rise smoothly out of the ground, before a vast green curtain. Now, a bell rings—a magic bell, which still sounds in my ears unlike all other bells—and music plays, amidst a buzz of voices, and a fragrant smell of orange-peel and oil. Anon, the magic bell commands the music to cease, and the great green curtain rolls itself up majestically, and The Play begins! The devoted dog of Montargis avenges the death of his master, foully murdered in the Forest of Bondy; and a humourous Peasant with a red nose and a very little hat, whom I take from this hour forth to my bosom as a friend (I think he was a Waiter or an Hostler at a village Inn, but many years have passed since he and I have met), remarks that the sassigassity of that dog is indeed surprising; and evermore this jocular conceit will live in my remembrance fresh and unfading, overtopping all possible jokes, unto the end of time. Or now, I learn with bitter tears how poor

Jane Shore, dressed all in white, and with her brown hair hanging down, went starving through the streets; or how George Barnwell killed the worthiest uncle that ever man had, and was afterwards so sorry for it that he ought to have been let off. Comes swift to comfort me, the Pantomime—stupendous Phenomenon!—when Clowns are shot from loaded mortars into the great chandelier, bright constellation that it is; when Harlequins, covered all over with scales of pure gold, twist and sparkle, like amazing fish; when Pantaloon (whom I deem it no irreverence to compare in my own mind to my grandfather) puts red-hot pokers in his pocket, and cries, "Here's somebody coming!" or taxes the Clown with petty larceny, by saying, "Now, I sawed you do it!" When Everything is capable, with the greatest of ease, of being changed into Anything; and "Nothing is, but thinking makes it so." Now, too, I perceive my first experience of the dreary sensation—often to return in after-life—of being unable, next day, to get back to the dull, settled world, of wanting to live forever in the bright atmosphere I have quitted; of doting on the little Fairy, with the wand like a celestial Barber's Pole, and pining for a Fairy immortality along with her. Ah! she comes back, in many shapes, as my eye wanders down the branches of my Christmas Tree, and goes as often, and has never yet stayed by me!

Out of this delight springs the toy theatre—there it is, with its familiar proscenium, and ladies in feathers, in the boxes!—and all its attendant occupation with paste and glue and gum, and water colours, in the getting up of The Miller and his Men, and Elizabeth, or the Exile of Siberia. In spite of a few besetting accidents and failures (particularly an unreasonable disposition in the respectable Kelmar, and some others, to become faint in the legs, and double up, at exciting points of the drama), a teeming world of fancies so suggestive and all-embracing, that, far below it on my Christmas Tree, I see dark, dirty, real Theatres in the daytime, adorned with these associations as with the freshest garlands of the rarest flowers, and charming me yet.

But hark! The Waits are playing, and they break my childish sleep! What images do I associate with the Christmas music as I see them set forth on the Christmas Tree? Known before all the others, keeping far apart from all the others, they gather round my little bed. An angel, speaking to a group of shepherds in a field; some travellers, with eyes uplifted, following a star; a baby in a manger; a child in a spacious temple, talking with grave men; a solemn figure, with a mild and beautiful face, raising a dead girl by the hand; again, near a city gate, calling back the son of a widow, on his bier, to life; a crowd of people looking through the opened roof of a chamber where he sits, and letting down a sick person on a bed, with ropes; the same, in a tempest, walking on the water to a ship; again, on a sea-shore, teaching a great multitude; again, with a child upon his knee, and other children round; again, restoring sight to the blind, speech to the dumb, hearing to the deaf, health to the sick, strength to the lame, knowledge to the ignorant; again, dying upon a cross, watched by armed soldiers, a thick darkness coming on, the earth beginning to shake, and only one voice heard. "Forgive them, for they know not what they do!"

Still, on the lower and maturer branches of the Tree, Christmas associations cluster thick. School-books shut up; Ovid and Virgil silenced; the Rule of Three, with its cool impertinent enquiries, long disposed of;

Terence and Plautus acted no more, in an arena of huddled desks and forms, all chipped, and notched, and inked; cricket-bats, stumps, and balls, left higher up, with the smell of trodden grass and the softened noise of shouts in the evening air; the tree is still fresh, still gay. If I no more come home at Christmas-time, there will be girls and boys (thank Heaven!) while the World lasts; and they do! Yonder they dance and play upon the branches of my Tree, God bless them, merrily, and my heart dances and plays too!

And I *do* come home at Christmas. We all do, or we all should. We all come home, or ought to come home, for a short holiday—the longer, the better—from the great boarding-school, where we are forever working at our arithmetical slates, to take, and give a rest. As to going a-visiting, where can we not go, if we will; where have we not been, when we would; starting our fancy away from our Christmas Tree!

Away into the winter prospect. There are many such upon the Tree! On, by low-lying misty grounds, through fens and fogs, up long hills, winding dark as caverns between thick plantations, almost shutting out the sparkling stars; so, out on broad heights, until we stop at last, with sudden silence, at an avenue. The gate-bell has a deep, half-awful sound in the frosty air; the gate swings open on its hinges; and, as we drive up to the great house, the glancing lights grow larger in the windows, and the opposing rows of trees seem to fall solemnly back on either side, to give us place. At intervals, all day, a frightened hare has shot across this whitened turf; or the distant clatter of a herd of deer trampling the hard frost, has, for the minute, crushed the silence too. Their watchful eyes beneath the fern may be shining now, if we could see them, like the icy dewdrops on the leaves; but they are still, and all is still. And so, the lights growing larger, and the trees falling back before us, and closing up again behind us, as if to forbid retreat, we come to the house.

There is probably a smell of roasted chestnuts and other good comfortable things all the time, for we are telling Winter Stories—Ghost Stories, or more shame for us—round the Christmas fire; and we have never stirred, except to draw a little nearer to it. But, no matter for that. We came to the house, and it is an old house, full of great chimneys where wood is burnt on ancient dogs upon the hearth, and grim portraits (some of them with grim legends, too) lower distrustfully from the oaken panels of the walls. We are a middle-aged nobleman, and we make a generous supper with our host and hostess and their guests—it being Christmastime, and the old house full of company—and then we go to bed. Our room is a very old room. It is hung with tapestry. We don't like the portrait of a cavalier in green, over the fireplace. There are great black beams in the ceiling, and there is a great black bedstead, supported at the foot by two great black figures, who seem to have come off a couple of tombs in the old baronial church in the park, for our particular accommodation. But we are not a superstitious nobleman, and we don't mind. Well! we dismiss our servant, lock the door, and sit before the fire in our dressing-gown, musing about a great many things. At length we go to bed. Well! we can't sleep. We toss and tumble, and can't sleep. The embers on the hearth burn fitfully and make the room look ghostly. We can't help peeping out over the counterpane, at the two black figures and the cavalier—that wicked-looking cavalier—in green. In the flickering light, they seem to advance and retire; which, though we are not by any means a superstitious nobleman, is not agreeable. Well! we get nervous—more and more nervous. We say, "This is very foolish, but we can't stand this; we'll pretend to be ill, and knock up somebody." Well! we are just going to do it, when the locked door opens, and there comes in a young woman, deadly pale, and with long fair hair, who glides to the fire, and sits down in the chair we have left there, wringing her hands. Then we notice that her clothes are wet. Our tongue cleaves to the roof of our mouth, and we can't speak; but we observe her accurately. Her clothes are wet; her long hair is dabbled with moist mud; she is dressed in the fashion of two hundred years ago; and she has at her girdle a bunch of rusty keys. Well! there she sits, and we can't even faint, we are in such a state about it. Presently she gets up, and tries all the locks in the room with the rusty keys, which won't fit one of them; then she fixes her eyes on the portrait of the cavalier in green, and says, in a low, terrible voice, "The stags know it!" After that, she wrings her hands again, passes the bedside, and goes out at the door. We hurry on our dressing-gown, seize our pistols (we always travel with pistols), and are following, when we find the door locked. We turn the key, look out into the dark gallery; no one there. We wander away, and try to find our servant. Can't be done. We pace the gallery till daybreak; then return to our deserted room, fall asleep, and are awakened by our servant (nothing ever haunts *him*) and the shining sun. Well! we make a wretched breakfast, and all the company say we look queer. After breakfast, we go over the house with our host, and then we take him to the portrait of the cavalier in green, and then it all comes out. He was false to a young housekeeper once attached to that family,

and famous for her beauty, who drowned herself in a
pond, and whose body was discovered, after a long
time, because the stags refused to drink of the water.
Since which, it has been whispered that she traverses
the house at midnight (but goes especially to that room
where the cavalier in green was wont to sleep), trying
the old locks with the rusty keys. Well! we tell our host
of what we have seen, and a shade comes over his features, and he begs it may be hushed up; and so it is.
But it's all true; and we said so, before we died (we are
dead now) to many responsible people.

There is no end to the old houses, with resounding
galleries, and dismal state-bed-chambers, and haunted
wings shut up for many years, through which we may
ramble, with an agreeable creeping up our back, and
encounter any number of ghosts, but (it is worthy of
remark perhaps) reducible to a very few general types
and classes; for, ghosts have little originality, and
"walk" in a beaten track. Thus, it comes to pass, that
a certain room in a certain old hall, where a certain
bad lord, baronet, knight, or gentleman, shot himself,
has certain planks in the floor from which the blood
will not be taken out. You may scrape and scrape, as
the present owner has done, or plane and plane, as
his father did, or scrub and scrub, as his grandfather
did, or burn and burn with strong acids, as his great-
grandfather did, but there the blood will still be—no
redder and no paler—no more and no less—always
just the same. Thus, in such another house there is a
haunted door, that never will keep open; or another
door that never will keep shut; or a haunted sound of
a spinning-wheel, or a hammer, or a footstep, or a cry,
or a sigh, or a horse's tramp, or the rattling of a chain.
Or else, there is a turret-clock, which, at the midnight

hour, strikes thirteen when the head of the family is going to die; or a shadowy, immovable black carriage which at such a time is always seen by somebody, waiting near the great gates in the stable-yard. Or thus, it came to pass how Lady Mary went to pay a visit at a large wild house in the Scottish Highlands, and, being fatigued with her long journey, retired to bed early, and innocently said, next morning, at the breakfast-table, "How odd, to have so late a party last night, in this remote place, and not to tell me of it, before I went to bed!" Then, every one asked Lady Mary what she meant? Then Lady Mary replied, "Why, all night long, the carriages were driving round and round the terrace, underneath my window!" Then the owner of the house turned pale, and so did his Lady, and Charles Macdoodle of Macdoodle signed to Lady Mary to say no more, and every one was silent. After breakfast, Charles Macdoodle told Lady Mary that it was a tradition in the family that those rumbling carriages on the terrace betokened death. And so it proved, for two months afterwards, the lady of the mansion died. And Lady Mary, who was a Maid of Honour at Court, often told this story to the old Queen Charlotte; by this token that the old King always said, "Eh, eh? What, what? Ghosts, ghosts? No such thing, no such thing!" And never left off saying so, until he went to bed.

Or, a friend of somebody's whom most of us know, when he was a young man at college, had a particular friend, with whom he made the compact that, if it were possible for the Spirit to return to this earth after its separation from the body, he of the twain who first died should reappear to the other. In course of time, this compact was forgotten by our friend; the two young men having progressed in life, and taken diverging paths that were wide asunder. But one night, many years afterwards, our friend being in the North of England, and staying for the night in an inn, on the Yorkshire Moors, happened to look out of bed; and there, in the moonlight, leaning on a bureau near the window, steadfastly regarding him, saw his old college friend! The appearance being solemnly addressed, replied, in a kind of whisper, but very audibly, "Do not come near me. I am dead. I am here to redeem my promise. I come from another world, but may not disclose its secrets!" Then, the whole form becoming paler, melted, as it were, into the moonlight, and faded away.

Or, there was the daughter of the first occupier of the picturesque Elizabethan house, so famous in our neighbourhood. You have heard about her? No! Why, *she* went out one summer evening, at twilight, when she was a beautiful girl, just seventeen years of age, to gather flowers in the garden; and presently came running, terrified, into the hall to her father, saying, "Oh, dear father, I have met myself!" He took her in his arms, and told her it was fancy, but she said, "Oh, no! I met myself in the broad walk, and I was pale and gathering withered flowers, and I turned my head, and held them up!" And that night she died, and a picture of her story was begun, though never finished, and they say it is somewhere in the house to this day, with its face to the wall.

Or, the uncle of my brother's wife was riding home on horseback, one mellow evening at sunset, when, in a green lane close to his own house, he saw a man standing before him, in the very centre of the narrow way. "Why does that man in the cloak stand there!" he thought. "Does he want me to ride over him?" But the figure never moved. He felt a strange sensation at seeing it so still, but slackened his trot and rode forward. When he was so close to it, as almost to touch it with his stirrup, his horse shied, and the figure glided up the bank, in a curious, unearthly manner—backward, and without seeming to use its feet—and was gone. The uncle of my brother's wife, exclaiming, "Good Heaven! It's my cousin Harry, from Bombay!" put spurs to his horse, which was suddenly in a profuse sweat, and, wondering at such strange behaviour, dashed round to the front of his house. There he saw the same figure, just passing in at the long French window of the drawing-room, opening on the ground. He threw his bridle to a servant, and hastened in after it. His sister was sitting there, alone. "Alice, where's my cousin Harry?" "Your cousin Harry, John?" "Yes. From Bombay. I met him in the lane just now, and saw him enter here, this instant." Not a creature had been seen by any one; and in that hour and minute, as it afterwards appeared, this cousin died in India.

Or, it was a certain sensible, old maiden lady, who died at ninety-nine, and retained her faculties to the last, who really did see the Orphan Boy; a story which has often been incorrectly told, but of which the real truth is this—because it is, in fact, a story belonging to our family—and she was a connection of our family. When she was about forty years of age, and still an uncommonly fine woman (her lover died young, which was the reason why she never married, though she had many offers), she went to stay at a place in Kent, which her brother, an Indian Merchant, had newly bought. There was a story that this place had once been held in trust, by the guardian of a young boy; who was himself the next heir, and who killed the young boy by harsh and cruel treatment. She knew nothing of that. It has been said that there was a Cage in her bedroom in which the guardian used to put the boy. There was no such thing. There was only a closet. She went to bed, made no alarm whatever in the night, and in the morning said composedly to her maid when she came in, "Who is the pretty forlorn-looking child who has been peeping out of that closet all night?" The maid replied by giving a loud scream, and instantly decamping. She was surprised; but she was a woman of remarkable strength of mind, and she dressed herself and went down-stairs, and closeted herself with her brother. "Now, Walter," she said, "I have been disturbed all night by a pretty forlorn-looking boy, who has been constantly peeping out of that closet in my room, which I can't open. This is some trick." "I am afraid not, Charlotte," said he, "for it is the legend of the house. It is the Orphan Boy. What did he do?" "He opened the door softly," said she, "and peeped out. Sometimes, he came a step or two into the room. Then I called to him, to encourage him, and he shrunk, and shuddered, and crept in again, and shut the door." "The closet has no communication, Charlotte," said her brother, "with any other part of the house, and it's nailed up." This was undeniably true, and it took two carpenters a whole forenoon to get it open for examination. Then she was satisfied that she had seen the Orphan Boy. But, the wild and terrible part of the story is, that he was also seen by three of her brother's sons, in succession, who all died young. On the occasion of each child being taken ill, he came home in a heat, twelve hours before, and said, Oh, mamma, he had been playing under a particular oak tree, in a certain meadow, with a strange boy—a pretty, forlorn-looking boy, who was very timid, and made signs! From fatal experience, the parents came to know that this was the Orphan Boy, and that the course of that child whom he chose for his little playmate was surely run.

Legion is the name of the German castles, where we sit up alone to wait for the Spectre—where we are shown into a room, made comparatively cheerful for our reception—where we glance round at the shadows, thrown on the blank walls by the crackling fire—where we feel very lonely when the village innkeeper and his pretty daughter have retired, after laying down a fresh store of wood upon the hearth, and setting forth on the small table such supper-cheer as a cold roast capon, bread, grapes, and a flask of old Rhine wine—where the reverberating doors close on their retreat, one after another, like so many peals of sullen thunder—and where, about the small hours of the night, we come into the knowledge of divers supernatural mysteries. Legion is the name of the haunted German students, in whose society we draw yet nearer to the fire, while the schoolboy in the corner opens his eyes wide and round, and flies off the footstool he has chosen for his seat, when the door accidentally blows open. Vast is the crop of such fruit, shining on our Christmas Tree; in blossom, almost at the very top; ripening all down the boughs!

Among the later toys and fancies hanging there—as idle often and less pure—be the images once associated with the sweet old Waits, the softened music in the night, ever unalterable! Encircled by the social thoughts of Christmas-time, still let the benignant figure of my childhood stand unchanged! In every cheerful image and suggestion that the season brings, may the bright star that rested above the poor roof be the star of all the Christian world! A moment's pause, O vanishing tree, of which the lower boughs are dark to me as yet, and let me look once more! I know there are blank spaces on thy branches, where eyes that I have loved, have shone and smiled; from which they are departed. But, far above, I see the raiser of the dead girl, and the Widow's Son; and God is good! If Age be hiding for me in the unseen portion of thy downward growth, oh! may I, with a grey head, turn a child's heart to that figure yet, and a child's trustfulness and confidence!

Now, the tree is decorated with bright merriment, and song, and dance, and cheerfulness. And they are welcome. Innocent and welcome be they ever held, beneath the branches of the Christmas Tree, which cast no gloomy shadow! But, as it sinks into the ground, I hear a whisper going through the leaves. "This, in commemoration of the law of love and kindness, mercy and compassion. This, in remembrance of Me!"

A
Christmas Dinner

(from *Sketches by Boz*)

❄❄❄❄❄❄❄❄❄❄❄❄❄❄

Christmas-time! That man must be a misanthrope indeed, in whose breast something like a jovial feeling is not roused—in whose mind some pleasant associations are not awakened—by the recurrence of Christmas. There are people who will tell you that Christmas is not to them what it used to be; that each succeeding Christmas has found some cherished hope, or happy prospect, of the year before, dimmed or passed away; that the present only serves to remind them of reduced circumstances and straitened incomes—of the feasts they once bestowed on hollow friends, and of the cold looks that meet them now, in adversity and misfortune. Never heed such dismal reminiscences. There are few men who have lived long enough in the world, who cannot call up such thoughts any day in the year. Then do not select the merriest of the three hundred and sixty-five for your doleful recollections, but draw your chair nearer the blazing fire—fill the glass and send round the song—and if your room be smaller than it was a dozen years ago, or if your glass be filled with reeking punch, instead of sparkling wine, put a good face on the matter, and empty it offhand, and fill another, and troll off the old ditty you used to sing, and thank God it's no worse. Look on the merry faces of your children (if you have any) as they sit round the fire. One little seat may be empty; one slight form that gladdened the father's heart, and roused the mother's pride to look upon, may not be there. Dwell not upon the past; think not that one short year ago, the fair child now resolving into dust, sat before you, with the bloom of health upon its cheek and the gaiety of infancy in its joyous eye. Reflect upon your present blessings—of which every man has many—not your misfortunes, of which all men have some. Fill your glass again, with a merry face and contented heart. Our life on it, but your Christmas shall be merry, and your new year a happy one!

Who can be insensible to the out-pourings of good feeling, and the honest interchange of affectionate attachment, which abound at this season of the year? A Christmas family-party! We know nothing in nature more delightful! There seems a magic in the very name of Christmas. Petty jealousies and discords are forgotten; social feelings are awakened, in bosoms to which they have long been strangers; father and son, or brother and sister, who have met and passed with averted gaze, or a look of cold recognition, for months before, proffer and return the cordial embrace, and bury their past animosities in their present happiness. Kindly hearts that have yearned towards each other, but have been withheld by false notions of pride and self-dignity, are again reunited, and all is kindness and benevolence! Would that Christmas lasted the whole year through (as it ought), and that the prejudices and passions which deform our better nature, were never called into action among those to whom they should ever be strangers!

The Christmas family-party that we mean, is not a mere assemblage of relations, got up at a week or two's notice, originating this year, having no family precedent in the last, and not likely to be repeated in the next. No. It is an annual gathering of all the accessible members of the family, young or old, rich or poor; and all the children look forward to it, for two months beforehand, in a fever of anticipation. Formerly it was held at grandpapa's; but grandpapa getting old, and grandmamma getting old too, and rather infirm, they have given up housekeeping, and domesticated themselves with uncle George; so, the party always takes place at uncle George's house, but grandmamma sends in most of the good things, and grandpapa always *will* toddle down, all the way to Newgate-market, to buy the turkey, which he engages a porter to bring home behind him in triumph, always insisting on the man's being rewarded with a glass of spirits, over and above his hire, to drink "a merry Christmas and a happy new year" to aunt George. As to grandmamma, she is very secret and mysterious for two or three days beforehand, but not sufficiently so to prevent rumours getting afloat that she has purchased a beautiful new cap with pink ribbons for each of the servants, together with sundry books, and pen-knives, and pencil-cases, for the younger branches; to say nothing of divers secret additions to the order originally given by aunt George at the pastry-cook's, such as another dozen of mince-pies for the dinner, and a large plum-cake for the children.

On Christmas Eve, grandmamma is always in excellent spirits, and after employing all the children during the day, in stoning the plums, and all that, insists, regularly every year, on uncle George coming down into the kitchen, taking off his coat, and stirring the pudding for half an hour or so, which uncle George good-humouredly does to the vociferous delight of the children and servants. The evening concludes with a glorious game of blind-man's buff, in an early stage of which grandpapa takes great care to be caught, in order that he may have an opportunity of displaying his dexterity.

On the following morning, the old couple, with as many of the children as the pew will hold, go to church in great state: leaving aunt George at home dusting decanters and filling castors, and uncle George carrying bottles into the dining-parlour, and calling for corkscrews, and getting into everybody's way.

When the church-party return to lunch, grandpapa produces a small sprig of mistletoe from his pocket, and tempts the boys to kiss their little cousins under it—a proceeding which affords both the boys and the old gentleman unlimited satisfaction, but which rather outrages grandmamma's ideas of decorum, until grandpapa says, that when he was just thirteen years and three months old, *he* kissed grandmamma under a mistletoe too, on which the children clap their hands, and laugh very heartily, as do aunt George and uncle George; and grandmamma looks pleased, and says, with a benevolent smile, that grandpapa was an impudent young dog, on which the children laugh very heartily again, and grandpapa more heartily than any of them.

But all these diversions are nothing to the subsequent excitement when grandmamma in a high cap, and slate-coloured silk gown; and grandpapa with a beautifully plaited shirt-frill, and white neckerchief; seat themselves on one side of the drawing-room fire, with uncle George's children and little cousins innumerable, seated in the front, waiting the arrival of the expected visitors. Suddenly a hackney-coach is heard to stop, and uncle George, who has been looking out of the window, exclaims, "Here's Jane!" on which the children rush to the door, and helter-skelter downstairs; and uncle Robert and aunt Jane, and the dear little baby, and the nurse, and the whole party, are ushered up-stairs amidst tumultuous shouts of "Oh, my!" from the children, and frequently repeated warnings not to hurt baby from the nurse. And grandpapa takes the child, and grandmamma kisses her daughter, and the confusion of this first entry has scarcely subsided, when some other aunts and uncles with more cousins arrive, and the grown-up cousins flirt with each other, and so do the little cousins too, for that matter, and nothing is to be heard but a confused din of talking, laughing, and merriment.

A hesitating double knock at the street-door, heard during a momentary pause in the conversation, excites a general inquiry of "Who's that?" and two or three children, who have been standing at the window, announce in a low voice, that it's "poor aunt Margaret." Upon which, aunt George leaves the room to welcome the new comer; and grandmamma draws herself up, rather stiff and stately; for Margaret married a poor man without her consent, and poverty not being a sufficient weighty punishment for her offence, has been discarded by her friends, and debarred the society of her dearest relatives. But Christmas has come round, and the unkind feelings that have struggled against better dispositions during the year, have melted away before its genial influence, like half-formed ice beneath the morning sun. It is not difficult in a moment of angry feeling for a parent to denounce a disobedient child; but, to banish her at a period of general good will and hilarity, from the hearth, round which she has sat on so many anniversaries of the same day, expanding by slow degrees from infancy to girlhood, and then bursting, almost imperceptibly, into a woman, is widely different. The air of conscious rectitude, and cold forgiveness, which the old lady has assumed, sits ill upon her; and when the poor girl is led in by her sister, pale in looks and broken in hope—not from poverty, for that she could bear, but from the consciousness of undeserved neglect, and unmerited unkindness—it is easy to see how much of it is assumed. A momentary pause succeeds; the girl breaks suddenly from her sister and throws herself, sobbing, on her mother's neck. The father steps hastily forward, and takes her husband's hand. Friends crowd round to offer their hearty congratulations, and happiness and harmony again prevail.

As to the dinner, it's perfectly delightful—nothing goes wrong, and everybody is in the very best of spirits, and disposed to please and be pleased. Grandpapa relates a circumstantial account of the purchase of the turkey, with a slight digression relative to the purchase of previous turkeys, on former Christmas Days, which grandmamma corroborates in the minutest particular. Uncle George tells stories, and carves poultry, and takes wine, and jokes with the children at the side-table, and winks at the cousins that are making love, or being made love to, and exhilarates everybody with his good humour and hospitality; and when, at last, a stout servant staggers in with a gigantic pudding, with a sprig of holly in the top, there is such a laughing, and shouting, and clapping of little chubby hands, and kicking up of fat dumpy legs, as can only be equalled by the applause with which the astonishing feat of pouring lighted brandy into mince-pies, is received by the younger visitors. Then the dessert!—and the wine!—and the fun! Such beautiful speeches, and *such* songs, from aunt Margaret's husband, who turns out to be such a nice man, and so attentive to grandmamma! Even grandpapa not only sings his annual song with unprecedented vigour, but on being honoured with an unanimous *encore*, according to annual custom, actually comes out with a new one which nobody but grandmamma ever heard before; and a young scapegrace of a cousin, who has been in some disgrace with the old people, for certain heinous sins of omission and commission—neglecting to call, and persisting in drinking Burton ale—astonishes everybody into convulsions of laughter by volunteering the most extraordinary comic songs that ever were heard. And thus the evening passes, in a strain of rational good-will and cheerfulness, doing more to awaken the sympathies of every member of the party in behalf of his neighbour, and to perpetuate their good feeling, during the ensuing year, than half the homilies that have ever been written, by half the Divines that have ever lived.

A Good-Humoured
Christmas

(from *The Pickwick Papers*)

✾ ✾ ✾ ✾ ✾ ✾ ✾ ✾ ✾ ✾ ✾ ✾ ✾ ✾ ✾

A good-humoured Christmas chapter, containing an account of a wedding, and some other sports beside, which, although in their way even as good customs as marriage itself, are not quite so religiously kept up in these degenerate times

As brisk as bees, if not altogether as light as fairies, did the four Pickwickians assemble on the morning of the twenty-second day of December, in the year of grace in which these, their faithfully recorded adventures, were undertaken and accomplished. Christmas was close at hand, in all his bluff and hearty honesty; it was the season of hospitality, merriment, and openheartedness; the old year was preparing, like an ancient philosopher, to call his friends around him and amidst the sound of feasting and revelry to pass gently and calmly away. Gay and merry was the time, and gay and merry were at least four of the numerous hearts that were gladdened by its coming.

And numerous indeed are the hearts to which

Christmas brings a brief season of happiness and enjoyment. How many families whose members have been dispersed and scattered far and wide, in the restless struggles of life, are then reunited, and meet once again in that happy state of companionship and mutual goodwill which is a source of such pure and unalloyed delight, and one so incompatible with the cares and sorrows of the world that the religious belief of the most civilized nations and the rude traditions of the roughest savages alike number it among the first joys of a future condition of existence provided for the blest and happy! How many old recollections and how many dormant sympathies does Christmas-time awaken!

We write these words now, many miles distant from the spot at which, year after year, we met on that day, a merry and joyous circle. Many of the hearts that throbbed so gaily then have ceased to beat; many of the looks that shone so brightly then have ceased to glow; the hands we grasped have grown cold; the eyes we sought have hid their lustre in the grave; and yet the old house, the room, the merry voices and smiling faces, the jest, the laugh, the most minute and trivial circumstances connected with those happy meetings, crowd upon our mind at each recurrence of the season, as if the last assemblage had been but yesterday! Happy, happy Christmas, that can win us back to the delusions of our childish days, that can recall to the old man the pleasures of his youth, that can transport the sailor and the traveller, thousands of miles away, back to his own fireside and his quiet home!

But we are so taken up and occupied with the good qualities of this saint Christmas that we are keeping Mr. Pickwick and his friends waiting in the cold on the outside of the Muggleton coach, which they have just attained, well wrapped up in great-coats, shawls, and comforters. The portmanteaus and carpet-bags have been stowed away, and Mr. Weller and the guard are endeavouring to insinuate into the fore-boot a huge cod-fish several sizes too large for it, which is snugly packed up in a long brown basket with a layer of straw over the top, and which has been left to the last, in order that he may repose in safety on the half-dozen barrels of real native oysters, all the property of Mr. Pickwick, which have been arranged in regular order at the bottom of the receptacle. The interest displayed in Mr. Pickwick's countenance is most intense as Mr. Weller and the guard try to squeeze the cod-fish into the boot, first head first, then tail first, and then top upward, and then bottom upward, and then sideways, and then long-ways, all of which artifices the implacable cod-fish sturdily resists until the guard accidentally hits him in the very middle of the basket, whereupon he suddenly disappears into the boot, and with him, the head and shoulders of the guard himself, who, not calculating upon so sudden a cessation of the passive resistance of the cod-fish, experiences a very unexpected shock, to the unsmotherable delight of all the porters and bystanders. Upon this, Mr. Pickwick smiles with great good humour, and drawing a shilling from his waistcoat pocket, begs the guard, as he picks himself out of the boot, to drink his health in a glass of hot brandy and water; at which the guard smiles too, and Messrs. Snodgrass, Winkle, and Tupman all smile in company. The guard and Mr. Weller disappear for five minutes; most probably to get the hot brandy and water, for they smell very strongly of it when they return; the coachman mounts to the box, Mr. Weller jumps up behind, the Pickwickians pull their coats round their legs and their shawls over their noses, the helpers pull the horse-cloths off, the coachman shouts out a cheery "All right," and away they go.

They have rumbled through the streets, and jolted over the stones, and at length reach the wide and open country. The wheels skim over the hard and frosty ground; and the horses, bursting into a canter at a smart crack of the whip, step along the road as if the load behind them—coach, passengers, cod-fish, oyster-barrels, and all—were but a feather at their heels. They have descended a gentle slope and enter upon a level, as compact and dry as a solid block of marble, two miles long. Another crack of the whip, and on they speed at a smart gallop, the horses tossing their heads and rattling the harness, as if in exhilaration at the rapidity of the motion, while the coachman, holding the whip and reins in one hand, takes off his hat with the other, and resting it on his knees, pulls out his handkerchief and wipes his forehead, partly because he has a habit of doing it and partly because it's as well to show the passengers how cool he is and what an easy thing it is to drive four-in-hand when you have had as much practice as he has. Having done this very leisurely (otherwise the effect would be materially impaired), he replaces his handkerchief, pulls on his hat, adjusts his gloves, squares his elbows, cracks the whip again, and on they speed, more merrily than before.

A few small houses scattered on either side of the road betoken the entrance to some town or village. The lively notes of the guard's key-bugle vibrate in the clear cold air and wake up the old gentleman inside, who, carefully letting down the window-sash half-way and standing sentry over the air, takes a short peep out and then, carefully pulling it up again, informs the other inside that they're going to change directly; on which the other inside wakes himself up and determines to postpone his next nap until after the stoppage. Again the bugle sounds lustily forth and rouses the cottager's wife and children, who peep out at the house-door and watch the coach till it turns the corner, when they once more crouch round the blazing fire and throw on another log of wood against father comes home; while father himself, a full mile off, has just exchanged a friendly nod with the coachman and turned round to take a good long stare at the vehicle as it whirls away.

And now the bugle plays a lively air as the coach rattles through the ill-paved streets of a country town; and the coachman, undoing the buckle which keeps his ribands together, prepares to throw them off the moment he stops. Mr. Pickwick emerges from his coat-collar and looks about him with great curiosity, perceiving which, the coachman informs Mr. Pickwick of the name of the town and tells him it was market-day yesterday, both of which pieces of information Mr. Pickwick retails to his fellow-passengers; whereupon they emerge from their coat-collars, too, and look about them also. Mr. Winkle, who sits at the extreme edge with one leg dangling in the air, is nearly precipitated into the street as the coach twists round the sharp corner by the cheesemonger's shop and turns into the market-place; and before Mr. Snodgrass, who sits next to him, has recovered from his alarm, they pull up at the inn-yard, where the fresh horses, with cloths on, are already waiting. The coachman throws down the reins and gets down himself, and the other outside passengers drop down also except those who have no great confidence in their ability to get up again; and they remain where they are and stamp their feet against the coach to warm them—looking, with longing eyes and red noses, at the bright fire in the inn-bar and the sprigs of holly with red berries which ornament the window.

But the guard has delivered at the corn-dealer's shop the brown-paper packet he took out of the little pouch which hangs over his shoulder by a leathern strap, and has seen the horses carefully put to, and has thrown on the pavement the saddle which was brought from London on the coach-roof, and has assisted in the conference between the coachman and the hostler about the gray mare that hurt her off-foreleg last Tuesday; and he and Mr. Weller are all right behind, and the coachman is all right in front, and the old gentleman inside, who has kept the window down full two inches all this time, has pulled it up again, and the cloths are off, and they are all ready for starting except the "two stout gentlemen," whom the coachman inquires after with some impatience. Hereupon the coachman, and the guard, and Sam Weller, and Mr. Winkle, and Mr. Snodgrass, and all the hostlers, and every one of the idlers, who are more in number than all the others put together, shout for the missing gentlemen as loud as they can bawl. A distant response is heard from the yard, and Mr. Pickwick and Mr. Tupman come running down it, quite out of breath, for they have been having a glass of ale apiece, and Mr. Pickwick's fingers are so cold that he has been full five minutes before he could find the sixpence to pay for it. The coachman shouts an admonitory "Now then, gen'lm'n!" The guard re-echoes it; the old gentleman inside thinks it a very extraordinary thing that people *will* get down when they know there isn't time for it; Mr. Pickwick struggles up on one side, Mr. Tupman on the other; Mr. Winkle cries, "All right"; and off they start. Shawls are pulled up, coat-collars are readjusted, the pavement ceases, the houses disappear, and they are once again dashing along the open road, with the fresh clear air blowing in their faces and gladdening their very hearts within them.

Such was the progress of Mr. Pickwick and his friends by the Muggleton telegraph on their way to Dingley Dell; and at three o'clock that afternoon they all stood, high and dry, safe and sound, hale and hearty, upon the steps of the Blue Lion, having taken on the road quite enough of ale and brandy to enable them to bid defiance to the frost that was binding up the earth in its iron fetters and weaving its beautiful network upon the trees and hedges. Mr. Pickwick was busily engaged in counting the barrels of oysters and superintending the disinterment of the cod-fish when he felt himself gently pulled by the skirts of the coat. Looking round, he discovered that the individual who resorted to this mode of catching his attention was no other than Mr. Wardle's favourite page, better known to the readers of this unvarnished history by the distinguishing appellation of the fat boy.

"Aha!" said Mr. Pickwick.

"Aha!" said the fat boy.

As he said it, he glanced from the cod-fish to the oyster-barrels and chuckled joyously. He was fatter than ever.

"Well, you look rosy enough, my young friend," said Mr. Pickwick.

"I've been asleep, right in front of the tap-room fire," replied the fat boy, who had heated himself to the colour of a new chimney-pot in the course of an hour's nap. "Master sent me over with the shay-cart to carry your luggage up to the house. He'd ha' sent some saddle-horses, but he thought you'd rather walk, being a cold day."

"Yes, yes," said Mr. Pickwick hastily, for he remembered how they had travelled over nearly the same ground on a previous occasion. "Yes, we would rather walk. Here, Sam!"

"Sir," said Mr. Weller.

"Help Mr. Wardle's servant to put the packages into the cart, and then ride on with him. We will walk forward at once."

Having given this direction and settled with the coachman, Mr. Pickwick and his three friends struck into the foot-path across the fields and walked briskly away, leaving Mr. Weller and the fat boy confronted together for the first time. Sam looked at the fat boy with great astonishment, but without saying a word, and began to stow the luggage rapidly away in the cart while the fat boy stood quietly by and seemed to think it a very interesting sort of thing to see Mr. Weller working by himself.

"There," said Sam, throwing in the last carpet-bag. "There they are!"

"Yes," said the fat boy in a very satisfied tone, "there they are."

"Vell, young twenty-stun," said Sam, "you're a nice specimen of a prize-boy, you are!"

"Thankee," said the fat boy.

"You ain't got nothin' on your mind as makes you fret yourself, have you?" inquired Sam.

"Not as I knows on," replied the fat boy.

"I should rayther ha' thought, to look at you, that

you was a-labourin' under an unrequited attachment to some young 'ooman," said Sam.

The fat boy shook his head.

"Vell," said Sam, "I'm glad to hear it. Do you ever drink anythin'?"

"I likes eating better," replied the boy.

"Ah," said Sam, "I should ha' s'posed that; but what I mean is, should you like a drop of anythin' as 'ud warm you? But I s'pose you never was cold, with all them elastic fixtures, was you?"

"Sometimes," replied the boy, "and I likes a drop of something when it's good."

"Oh, you do, do you?" said Sam. "Come this way, then!"

The Blue Lion tap was soon gained, and the fat boy swallowed a glass of liquor without so much as winking, a feat which considerably advanced him in Mr. Weller's good opinion. Mr. Weller having transacted a similar piece of business on his own account, they got into the cart.

"Can you drive?" said the fat boy.

"I should rayther think so," replied Sam.

"There, then," said the fat boy, putting the reins in his hand and pointing up a lane, "it's as straight as you can go; you can't miss it."

With these words, the fat boy laid himself affectionately down by the side of the cod-fish, and placing an oyster-barrel under his head for a pillow, fell asleep instantaneously.

"Well," said Sam, "of all the cool boys ever I set my eyes on, this here young gen'lm'n is the coolest. Come, wake up, young dropsy!"

But as young dropsy evinced no symptoms of returning animation, Sam Weller sat himself down in front of the cart, and starting the old horse with a jerk of the rein, jogged steadily on towards Manor Farm.

Meanwhile, Mr. Pickwick and his friends, having walked their blood into active circulation, proceeded cheerfully on. The paths were hard; the grass was crisp and frosty; the air had a fine, dry, bracing coldness; and the rapid approach of the grey twilight (slate-coloured is a better term in frosty weather) made them look forward with pleasant anticipation to the comforts which awaited them at their hospitable entertainer's. It was the sort of afternoon that might induce a couple of elderly gentlemen, in a lonely field, to take off their great-coats and play at leap-frog in pure lightness of heart and gaiety; and we firmly believe that had Mr. Tupman at that moment proffered "a back," Mr. Pickwick would have accepted his offer with the utmost avidity.

However, Mr. Tupman did not volunteer any such accommodation, and the friends walked on, conversing merrily. As they turned into a lane they had to cross, the sound of many voices burst upon their ears; and before they had even had time to form a guess to whom they belonged, they walked into the very centre of the party who were expecting their arrival—a fact which was first notified to the Pickwickians by the loud "Hurrah" which burst from old Wardle's lips when they appeared in sight.

First, there was Wardle himself, looking, if possible, more jolly than ever; then there were Bella and her faithful Trundle; and, lastly, there were Emily and some eight or ten young ladies, who had all come down to the wedding, which was to take place next day, and who were in as happy and important a state as young ladies usually are on such momentous occasions; and they were, one and all, startling the fields and lanes, far and wide, with their frolic and laughter.

The ceremony of introduction under such circumstances was very soon performed, or we should rather say that the introduction was soon over without any ceremony at all. In two minutes thereafter, Mr. Pickwick was joking with the young ladies who wouldn't come over the stile while he looked—or who, having pretty feet and unexceptionable ankles, preferred standing on the top rail for five minutes or so, declaring that they were too frightened to move—with as much ease and absence of reserve or constraint as if he had known them for life. It is worthy of remark, too, that Mr. Snodgrass offered Emily far more assistance than the absolute terrors of the stile (although it was full three feet high and had only a couple of stepping-stones) would seem to require; while one black-eyed young lady, in a very nice little pair of boots with fur round the top, was observed to scream very loudly when Mr. Winkle offered to help her over.

All this was very snug and pleasant. And when the difficulties of the stile were at last surmounted, and they once more entered on the open field, old Wardle informed Mr. Pickwick how they had all been down in a body to inspect the furniture and fittings-up of the house which the young couple were to tenant after the Christmas holidays; at which communication, Bella and Trundle both coloured up as red as the fat boy after the tap-room fire; and the young lady with the black eyes and the fur round the boots whispered something in Emily's ear and then glanced archly at Mr. Snodgrass, to which Emily responded that she was a foolish girl, but turned very red notwithstanding; and Mr. Snodgrass, who was as modest as all great geniuses usually are, felt the crimson rising to the crown of his head, and devoutly wished in the inmost recesses of his own heart that the young lady aforesaid with her black eyes, and her archness, and her boots with the fur round the top were all comfortably deposited in the adjacent county.

But if they were social and happy outside the house, what was the warmth and cordiality of their reception when they reached the farm! The very servants grinned with pleasure at sight of Mr. Pickwick; and Emma bestowed a half-demure, half-impudent, and all-pretty look of recognition on Mr. Tupman, which was enough to make the statue of Bonaparte in the passage unfold his arms and clasp her within them.

The old lady was seated in customary state in the front parlour, but she was rather cross and, by consequence, most particularly deaf. She never went out herself, and like a great many other old ladies of the same stamp, she was apt to consider it an act of domestic treason if anybody else took the liberty of doing what she couldn't. So, bless her old soul, she sat as upright as she could in her great chair and looked as fierce as might be—and that was benevolent, after all.

"Mother," said Wardle, "Mr. Pickwick. You recollect him?"

"Never mind," replied the old lady with great dignity. "Don't trouble Mr. Pickwick about an old creetur like me. Nobody cares about me now, and it's very nat'ral they shouldn't." Here the old lady tossed her head, and smoothed down her lavender-coloured silk dress with trembling hands.

"Come, come, ma'am," said Mr. Pickwick, "I can't let you cut an old friend in this way. I have come down expressly to have a long talk and another rubber with you; and we'll show these boys and girls how to dance a minuet before they're eight-and-forty hours older."

The old lady was rapidly giving way, but she did not like to do it all at once; so she only said, "Ah! I can't hear him!"

"Nonsense, Mother," said Wardle. "Come, come, don't be cross, there's a good soul. Recollect Bella; come, you must keep her spirits up, poor girl."

The good old lady heard this, for her lip quivered as her son said it. But age has its little infirmities of temper, and she was not quite brought round yet. So, she smoothed down the lavender-coloured dress again and, turning to Mr. Pickwick, said, "Ah, Mr. Pickwick, young people was very different when I was a girl."

"No doubt of that, ma'am," said Mr. Pickwick, "and that's the reason why I would make much of the few that have any traces of the old stock"; and saying this, Mr. Pickwick gently pulled Bella towards him and, bestowing a kiss upon her forehead, bade her sit down on the little stool at her grandmother's feet. Whether the expression of her countenance, as it was raised towards the old lady's face, called up a thought of old times, or whether the old lady was touched by Mr. Pickwick's affectionate good nature, or whatever was the cause, she was fairly melted; so she threw herself on her granddaughter's neck, and all the little ill humour evaporated in a gush of silent tears.

A happy party they were that night. Sedate and solemn were the score of rubbers in which Mr. Pickwick and the old lady played together; uproarious was the mirth of the round table. Long after the ladies had retired did the hot elder-wine, well qualified with brandy and spice, go round and round and round again; and sound was the sleep and pleasant were the dreams that followed It is a remarkable fact that those of Mr. Snodgrass bore constant reference to Emily Wardle, and that the principal figure in Mr. Winkle's visions was a young lady with black eyes, an arch smile, and a pair of remarkably nice boots with fur round the tops.

Mr. Pickwick was awakened early in the morning by a hum of voices and a pattering of feet, sufficient to rouse even the fat boy from his heavy slumbers. He sat up in bed and listened. The female servants and female visitors were running constantly to and fro; and there were such multitudinous demands for hot water, such repeated outcries for needles and thread, and so many half-suppressed entreaties of "Oh, do come and tie me, there's a dear!" that Mr. Pickwick in his innocence began to imagine that something dreadful must have occurred, when he grew more awake and remembered the wedding. The occasion being an important one, he dressed himself with peculiar care and descended to the breakfast-room.

There were all the female servants, in a brand-new uniform of pink muslin gowns with white bows in their caps, running about the house in a state of excitement and agitation which it would be impossible to describe. The old lady was dressed out in a brocaded gown which had not seen the light for twenty years saving and excepting such truant rays as had stolen through the chinks in the box in which it had been lain by during the whole time. Mr. Trundle was in high feather and spirits, but a little nervous withal. The hearty old landlord was trying to look very cheerful and unconcerned, but failing signally in the attempt. All the girls were in tears and white muslin except a select two or three who were being honoured with a private view of the bride and bridesmaids up-stairs. All the Pickwickians were in most blooming array; and there was a terrific roaring on the grass in front of the house, occasioned by all the men, boys, and hobble-dehoys attached to the farm, each of whom had got a white bow in his button-hole, and all of whom were cheering with might and main, being incited thereunto and stimulated therein by the precept and example of Mr. Samuel Weller, who had managed to become mighty popular already and was as much at home as if he had been born on the land.

A wedding is a licensed subject to joke upon, but there really is no great joke in the matter after all; we speak merely of the ceremony, and beg it to be distinctly understood that we indulge in no hidden sarcasm upon a married life. Mixed up with the pleasure and joy of the occasion are the many regrets at quitting home, the tears of parting between parent and child, the consciousness of leaving the dearest and kindest friends of the happiest portion of human life, to encounter its cares and troubles with others still untried and little known—natural feelings which we would not render this chapter mournful by describing and which we should be still more unwilling to be supposed to ridicule.

Let us briefly say, then, that the ceremony was performed by the old clergyman, in the parish church of Dingley Dell, and that Mr. Pickwick's name is attached to the register, still preserved in the vestry thereof; that the young lady with the black eyes signed her name in a very unsteady and tremulous manner; that Emily's signature, as the other bridesmaid, is nearly illegible; that it all went off in very admirable style; that the young ladies generally thought it far less shocking than they had expected; and that although the owner of the black eyes and the arch smile informed Mr. Winkle that she was sure she could never submit to anything so dreadful, we have the very best reasons for thinking she was mistaken. To all this we may add that Mr. Pickwick was the first who saluted the bride, and that in so doing, he threw over her neck a rich gold watch and chain, which no mortal eyes but the jeweller's had ever beheld before. Then, the old church-bell rang as gaily as it could, and they all returned to breakfast.

"Vere does the mince-pies go, young opium-eater?" said Mr. Weller to the fat boy as he assisted in laying out such articles of consumption as had not been duly arranged on the previous night.

The fat boy pointed to the destination of the pies.

"Wery good," said Sam, "stick a bit o' Christmas in 'em. T'other dish opposite. There; now we look compact and comfortable, as the father said ven he cut his little boy's head off to cure him o' squintin'."

As Mr. Weller made the comparison, he fell back a step or two, to give full effect to it, and surveyed the preparations with the utmost satisfaction.

"Wardle," said Mr. Pickwick almost as soon as they were all seated, "a glass of wine in honour of this happy occasion!"

"I shall be delighted, my boy," said Wardle. "Joe—damn that boy, he's gone to sleep."

"No, I ain't, sir," replied the fat boy, starting up from a remote corner where, like the patron saint of fat boys—the immortal Horner—he had been devouring a Christmas-pie, though not with the coolness and deliberation which characterized that young gentleman's proceedings.

"Fill Mr. Pickwick's glass."

"Yes, sir."

The fat boy filled Mr. Pickwick's glass and then retired behind his master's chair, from whence he watched the play of the knives and forks, and the progress of the choice morsels from the dishes to the mouths of the company, with a kind of dark and gloomy joy that was most impressive.

"God bless you, old fellow!" said Mr. Pickwick.

"Same to you, my boy," replied Wardle; and they pledged each other heartily.

"Mrs. Wardle," said Mr. Pickwick, "we old folks must have a glass of wine together in honour of this joyful event."

The old lady was in a state of great grandeur just then, for she was sitting at the top of the table in the brocaded gown, with her newly married granddaughter on one side and Mr. Pickwick on the other, to do the carving. Mr. Pickwick had not spoken in a very loud tone, but she understood him at once and drank off a full glass of wine to his long life and happiness; after which the worthy old soul launched forth into a minute and particular account of her own wedding, with a dissertation on the fashion of wearing high-heeled shoes, and some particulars concerning the life and adventures of the beautiful Lady Tollimglower, deceased; at all of which, the old lady herself laughed very heartily, indeed, and so did the young ladies too, for they were wondering among themselves what on earth Grandma was talking about. When they laughed, the old lady laughed ten times more heartily and said that these always had been considered capital stories, which caused them all to laugh again, and put the old lady into the very best of humours. Then the cake was cut and passed through the ring; the young ladies saved pieces to put under their pillows to dream of their future husbands on; and a great deal of blushing and merriment was thereby occasioned.

"Mr. Miller," said Mr. Pickwick to his old acquaintance the hard-headed gentleman, "a glass of wine?"

"With great satisfaction, Mr. Pickwick," replied the hard-headed gentleman solemnly.

"You'll take me in?" said the benevolent old clergyman.

"And me," interposed his wife.

"And me, and me," said a couple of poor relations at the bottom of the table, who had eaten and drank very heartily and laughed at everything.

Mr. Pickwick expressed his heart-felt delight at every additional suggestion, and his eyes beamed with hilarity and cheerfulness.

"Ladies and gentlemen," said Mr. Pickwick, suddenly rising.

"Hear, hear! Hear, hear! Hear, hear!" cried Mr. Weller in the excitement of his feelings.

"Call in all the servants," cried old Wardle, interposing to prevent the public rebuke which Mr. Weller would otherwise most indubitably have received from his master. "Give them a glass of wine each, to drink the toast in. Now, Pickwick."

Amidst the silence of the company, the whispering of the women-servants, and the awkward embarrassment of the men, Mr. Pickwick proceeded.

"Ladies and gentlemen—no, I won't say ladies and gentlemen, I'll call you my friends—my dear friends, if the ladies will allow me to take so great a liberty—"

Here Mr. Pickwick was interrupted by immense applause from the ladies, echoed by the gentlemen, during which the owner of the eyes was distinctly heard to state that she could kiss that dear Mr. Pickwick. Whereupon Mr. Winkle gallantly inquired if it couldn't be done by deputy, to which the young lady with the black eyes replied, "Go away," and accompanied the request with a look which said as plainly as a look could do: "if you can."

"My dear friends," resumed Mr. Pickwick, "I am going to propose the health of the bride and the bridegroom—God bless 'em" (cheers and tears). "My young friend Trundle I believe to be a very excellent and manly fellow; and his wife I know to be a very amiable and lovely girl, well qualified to transfer to another sphere of action the happiness which for twenty years she has diffused around her in her father's house." (Here the fat boy burst forth into stentorian blubberings, and was led forth by the coat-collar by Mr. Weller.) "I wish," added Mr. Pickwick, "I wish I was young enough to be her sister's husband" (cheers), "but failing that, I am happy to be old enough to be her father; for, being so, I shall not be suspected of any latent designs when I say that I admire, esteem, and love them both" (cheers and sobs). "The bride's father, our good friend there, is a noble person, and I am proud to know him" (great uproar). "He is a kind, excellent, independent-spirited, fine-hearted, hospitable, liberal man" (enthusiastic shouts from the poor relations at all the adjectives, and especially at the two last). "That his daughter may enjoy all the happiness even he can desire, and that he may derive from the contemplation of her felicity all the gratification of heart and peace of mind which he so well deserves, is, I am persuaded, our united wish. So, let us drink their healths and wish them prolonged life and every blessing!"

Mr. Pickwick concluded amidst a whirlwind of applause; and once more were the lungs of the supernumeraries, under Mr. Weller's command, brought into active and efficient operation. Mr. Wardle proposed Mr. Pickwick; Mr. Pickwick proposed the old lady. Mr. Snodgrass proposed Mr. Wardle; Mr. Wardle proposed Mr. Snodgrass. One of the poor relations proposed Mr. Tupman, and the other poor relation proposed Mr. Winkle; all was happiness and festivity until the mysterious disappearance of both the poor relations beneath the table warned the party that it was time to adjourn.

At dinner they met again, after a five-and-twenty-mile walk, undertaken by the males at Wardle's recommendation, to get rid of the effects of the wine at breakfast. The poor relations had kept in bed all day, with the view of attaining the same happy consummation, but as they had been unsuccessful, they stopped there. Mr. Weller kept the domestics in a state of perpetual hilarity; and the fat boy divided his time into small alternate allotments of eating and sleeping.

The dinner was as hearty an affair as the breakfast, and was quite as noisy, without the tears. Then came the dessert and some more toasts. Then came the tea and coffee, and then the ball.

The best sitting-room at Manor Farm was a good, long, dark-panelled room with a high chimney-piece and a capacious chimney, up which you could have driven one of the new patent cabs, wheels and all. At the upper end of the room, seated in a shady bower of holly and evergreens, were the two best fiddlers and the only harp in all Muggleton. In all sorts of recesses, and on all kinds of brackets, stood massive old silver candlesticks with four branches each. The carpet was up, the candles burnt bright, the fire blazed and crackled on the hearth, and merry voices and light-hearted laughter rang through the room. If any of the old English yeomen had turned into fairies when they died, it was just the place in which they would have held their revels.

If anything could have added to the interest of this agreeable scene, it would have been the remarkable fact of Mr. Pickwick's appearing without his gaiters, for the first time within the memory of his oldest friends.

"You mean to dance?" said Wardle.

"Of course I do," replied Mr. Pickwick. "Don't you see I am dressed for the purpose?" Mr. Pickwick called attention to his speckled silk stockings and smartly tied pumps.

"*You* in silk stockings!" exclaimed Mr. Tupman jocosely.

"And why not, sir—why not?" said Mr. Pickwick, turning warmly upon him.

"Oh, of course there is no reason why you shouldn't wear them," responded Mr. Tupman.

"I imagine not, sir, I imagine not," said Mr. Pickwick in a very peremptory tone.

Mr. Tupman had contemplated a laugh, but he found it was a serious matter; so he looked grave and said they were a pretty pattern.

"I hope they are," said Mr. Pickwick, fixing his eyes upon his friend. "You see nothing extraordinary in the stockings *as* stockings, I trust sir?"

"Certainly not. Oh, certainly not," replied Mr. Tupman. He walked away, and Mr. Pickwick's countenance resumed its customary benign expression.

"We are all ready, I believe," said Mr. Pickwick, who was stationed with the old lady at the top of the dance, and had already made four false starts in his excessive anxiety to commence.

"Then begin at once," said Wardle. "Now!"

Up struck the two fiddles and the one harp, and off went Mr. Pickwick into hands across, when there was a general clapping of hands and a cry of "Stop, stop!"

"What's the matter?" said Mr. Pickwick, who was only brought to by the fiddles and harp desisting, and could have been stopped by no other earthly power if the house had been on fire.

"Where's Arabella Allen?" cried a dozen voices.

"And Winkle?" added Mr. Tupman.

"Here we are!" exclaimed that gentleman, emerging with his pretty companion from the corner; as he did so it would have been hard to tell which was the redder in the face, he or the young lady with the black eyes.

"What an extraordinary thing it is, Winkle," said Mr. Pickwick rather pettishly, "that you couldn't have taken your place before."

"Not at all extraordinary," said Mr. Winkle.

"Well," said Mr. Pickwick with a very expressive smile as his eyes rested on Arabella, "well, I don't know that it *was* extraordinary either, after all."

However, there was no time to think more about the matter, for the fiddles and harp began in real earnest. Away went Mr. Pickwick—hands across—down the middle to the very end of the room, and half-way up the chimney, back again to the door—poussette everywhere—loud stamp on the ground—ready for the next couple—off again—all the figure over once more—another stamp to beat out the time—next couple, and the next, and the next again—never was such going! At last, after they had reached the bottom of the dance, and full fourteen couple after the old lady had retired in an exhausted state, and the clergyman's wife had been substituted in her stead, did that gentleman, when there was no demand whatever on his exertions, keep perpetually dancing in his place to keep time to the music; smiling on his partner all the while with a blandness of demeanour which baffles all description.

Long before Mr. Pickwick was weary of dancing, the newly married couple had retired from the scene. There was a glorious supper downstairs notwithstanding, and a good long sitting after it; and when Mr. Pickwick awoke, late the next morning, he had a confused recollection of having, severally and confidentially, invited somewhere about five-and-forty people to dine with him at the George and Vulture the very first time they came to London, which Mr. Pickwick rightly considered a pretty certain indication of his having taken something besides exercise on the previous night.

"And so your family has games in the kitchen tonight, my dear, has they?" inquired Sam of Emma.

"Yes, Mr. Weller," replied Emma; "we always have on Christmas Eve. Master wouldn't neglect to keep it up on any account."

"Your master's a wery pretty notion of keepin' anythin' up, my dear," said Mr. Weller; "I never see such a sensible sort of man as he is or such a reg'lar gen'lm'n."

"Oh, that he is!" said the fat boy, joining in the conversation. "Don't he breed nice pork!" The fat youth gave a semi-cannibalic leer at Mr. Weller as he thought of the roast legs and gravy.

"Oh, you've woke up at last, have you?" said Sam.

The fat boy nodded.

"I'll tell you what it is, young boa-constructer," said Mr. Weller impressively; "if you don't sleep a little less and exercise a little more, wen you comes to be a man, you'll lay yourself open to the same sort of personal inconwenience as was inflicted on the old gen'lm'n as wore the pigtail."

"What did they do to him?" inquired the fat boy in a faltering voice.

"I'm a-goin' to tell you," replied Mr. Weller; "he was one o' the largest patterns as was ever turned out— reg'lar fat man as hadn't caught a glimpse of his own shoes for five-and-forty year."

"Lor'!" exclaimed Emma.

"No, that he hadn't, my dear," said Mr. Weller; "and if you'd put an exact model of his own legs on the dinin'-table afore him, he wouldn't ha' known 'em. Well, he always walks to his office with a wery handsome gold watch-chain hanging out about a foot and a quarter, and a gold watch in his fob pocket as was worth—I'm afraid to say how much, but as much as a watch can be—a large, heavy, round manafacter, as stout for a watch as he was for a man, and with a big face in proportion. 'You'd better not carry that 'ere watch,' says the old gen'lm'n's friends, 'you'll be robbed of it,' says they. 'Shall I?' says he. 'Yes, you will,' says they. 'Vell,' says he, 'I should like to see the thief as could get this here watch out for I'm blest if *I* ever can, it's such a tight fit,' says he; 'and venever I wants to know what's o'clock, I'm obliged to stare into the bakers' shops,' he says. Well, then he laughs as hearty as if he was a-goin' to pieces, and out he walks agin with his powdered head and pigtail, and rolls down the Strand vith the chain hangin' out furder than ever and the great round watch almost bustin' through his grey kersey smalls. There warn't a pickpocket in all London as didn't take a pull at that chain, but the chain 'ud never break, and the watch 'ud never come out, so they soon got tired o' dragging such a heavy old gen'lm'n along the pavement, and he'd go home and laugh till the pigtail wibrated like the pendulum of a Dutch clock. At last, one day the old gen'lm'n was a-rollin' along, and he sees a pickpocket as he knowed by sight a-comin' up arm-in-arm with a little boy vith a wery large head. 'Here's a game,' says the old gen'lm'n to himself; 'they're a-goin' to have another try, but it won't do!' So he begins a-chucklin' wery hearty wen, all of a sudden, the little boy leaves hold of the pickpocket's arm and rushes head-foremost straight into the old gen'lm'n's stomach, and, for a moment doubles him right up vith the pain. 'Murder!' says the old gen'lm'n. 'All right, sir,' says the pickpocket, a-whisperin' in his ear. And wen he come straight agin, the watch and chain was gone, and what's worse than that, the old gen'lm'n's digestion was all wrong ever artervards, to the wery last day of his life; so just you look about you, young feller, and take care you don't get too fat."

As Mr. Weller concluded this moral tale, with which the fat boy appeared much affected, they all three repaired to the large kitchen, in which the family were by this time assembled, according to annual custom on Christmas Eve, observed by old Wardle's forefathers from time immemorial.

From the centre of the ceiling of this kitchen, old Wardle had just suspended with his own hands a huge branch of mistletoe, and this same branch of mistletoe instantaneously gave rise to a scene of general and most delightful struggling and confusion; in the midst of which, Mr. Pickwick, with a gallantry that would have done honour to a descendant of Lady Tollimglower herself, took the old lady by the hand, led her beneath the mystic branch, and saluted her in all courtesy and decorum. The old lady submitted to this piece of practical politeness with all the dignity which befitted so important and serious a solemnity, but the younger ladies, not being so thoroughly imbued with a superstitious veneration for the custom—or imagining that the value of a salute is very much enhanced if it cost a little trouble to obtain it—screamed and struggled, and ran into corners, and threatened and remonstrated, and did everything but leave the room until some of the less adventurous gentlemen were on the point of desisting when they all at once found it useless to resist any longer and submitted to be kissed with good grace. Mr. Winkle kissed the young lady with the black eyes, and Mr. Snodgrass kissed Emily, and Mr. Weller, not being particular about the form of being under the mistletoe, kissed Emma and the other female servants just as he caught them. As to the poor relations, they kissed everybody, not even excepting the plainer portions of the young-lady visitors, who, in their excessive confusion, ran right under the mistletoe, as soon as it was hung up, without knowing it! Wardle stood with his back to the fire, surveying the whole scene with the utmost satisfaction; and the fat boy took the opportunity of appropriating to his own use, and summarily devouring, a particularly fine mince-pie that had been carefully put by for somebody else.

Now, the screaming had subsided, and faces were in a glow, and curls in a tangle, and Mr. Pickwick, after kissing the old lady, as before mentioned, was standing under the mistletoe, looking with a very pleased countenance on all that was passing around him, when the young lady with the black eyes, after a little whispering with the other young ladies, made a sudden dart forward and, putting her arm round Mr. Pickwick's neck, saluted him affectionately on the left cheek; and before Mr. Pickwick distinctly knew what was the matter, he was surrounded by the whole body and kissed by every one of them.

It was a pleasant thing to see Mr. Pickwick in the centre of the group, now pulled this way, and then that, and first kissed on the chin, and then on the nose, and then on the spectacles, and to hear the peals of laughter which were raised on every side; but it was a still more pleasant thing to see Mr. Pickwick, blinded shortly afterwards with a silk handkerchief, falling up against the wall, and scrambling into corners, and going through all the mysteries of blind-man's-buff, with the utmost relish for the game, until at last he caught one of the poor relations and then had to evade the blind-man himself, which he did with a nimbleness and agility that elicited the admiration and applause of all beholders. The poor relations caught the people who they thought would like it, and when the game flagged, got caught themselves. When they were all tired of blind-man's buff, there was a great game at snapdragon, and when fingers enough were burned with that, and all the raisins were gone, they sat down by the huge fire of blazing logs to a substantial supper and a mighty bowl of wassail, something smaller than an ordinary washhouse copper, in which the hot apples were hissing and bubbling with a rich look and a jolly sound that were perfectly irresistible.

"This," said Mr. Pickwick, looking round him, "this is, indeed, comfort."

"Our invariable custom," replied Mr. Wardle. "Everybody sits down with us on Christmas Eve, as you see them now—servants and all; and here we wait, until the clock strikes twelve, to usher Christmas in, and beguile the time with forfeits and old stories. Trundle, my boy, rake up the fire."

Up flew the bright sparks in myriads as the logs were stirred. The deep red blaze sent forth a rich glow that penetrated into the furthest corner of the room and cast its cheerful tint on every face.

"Come," said Wardle, "a song—a Christmas song! I'll give you one in default of a better."

"Bravo!" said Mr. Pickwick.

"Fill up," cried Wardle. "It will be two hours, good, before you see the bottom of the bowl through the deep rich colour of the wassail; fill up all round, and now for the song."

Thus saying, the merry old gentleman, in a good, round, sturdy voice, commenced without more ado:

A CHRISTMAS CAROL

"I CARE not for Spring, on his fickle wing
Let the blossoms and buds be borne;
He woos them amain with his treacherous rain,
And he scatters them ere the morn.
An inconstant elf, he knows not himself,
Nor his own changing mind an hour,
He'll smile in your face, and, with wry grimace,
He'll wither your youngest flower.

"Let the Summer sun to his bright home run,
He shall never be sought by me;
When he's dimmed by a cloud I can laugh aloud,
And care not how sulky he be!
For his darling child is the madness wild

That sports in fierce fever's train;
And when love is too strong, it don't last long,
As many have found to their pain.

"A mild harvest night, by the tranquil light
Of the modest and gentle moon,
Has far sweeter sheen, for me, I ween,
Than the broad and unblushing noon.
But every leaf awakens my grief,
As it lieth beneath the tree;
So let Autumn air be never so fair,
It by no means agrees with me.

"But my song I troll out, for CHRISTMAS stout,
The hearty, the true, and the bold;
A bumper I drain, and with might and main
Give three cheers for this Christmas old!
We'll usher him in with a merry din
That shall gladden his joyous heart,
And we'll keep him up, while there's bite or sup,
And in fellowship good, we'll part.

"In his fine honest pride, he scorns to hide
One jot of his hard-weather scars;
They're no disgrace, for there's much the same trace
On the cheeks of our bravest tars.
Then again I sing till the roof doth ring,
And it echoes from wall to wall—
To the stout old wight, fair welcome to-night,
As the King of the Seasons all!"

This song was tumultuously applauded—for friends
and dependents make a capital audience—and the poor

relations, especially, were in perfect ecstasies of rapture. Again was the fire replenished, and again went the wassail round.

"How it snows!" said one of the men in a low tone.

"Snow, does it?" said Wardle.

"Rough, cold night, sir," replied the man; "and there's a wind got up that drifts it across the fields in a thick white cloud."

"What does Jem say?" inquired the old lady. "There ain't anything the matter, is there?"

"No, no, Mother," replied Wardle; "he says there's a snow-drift and a wind that's piercing cold. I should know that, by the way it rumbles in the chimney."

"Ah!" said the old lady. "There was just such a wind and just such a fall of snow, a good many years back, I recollect—just five years before your poor father died. It was a Christmas Eve, too; and I remember that on that very night, he told us the story about the goblins that carried away old Gabriel Grub."

"The story about what?" said Mr. Pickwick.

"Oh, nothing, nothing," replied Wardle. "About an old sexton that the good people down here suppose to have been carried away by goblins."

"Suppose!" ejaculated the old lady. "Is there anybody hardy enough to disbelieve it? Suppose! Haven't you heard, ever since you were a child, that he *was* carried away by the goblins, and don't you know he was?"

"Very well, Mother, he was, if you like," said Wardle, laughing. "He *was* carried away by goblins, Pickwick; and there's an end of the matter."

"No, no," said Mr. Pickwick, "not an end of it, I assure you; for I must hear how and why and all about it."

Wardle smiled as every head was bent forward to hear, and filling out the wassail with no stinted hand, nodded a health to Mr. Pickwick and began as follows:

But bless our editorial heart, what a long chapter we have been betrayed into! We had quite forgotten all such petty restrictions as chapters, we solemnly declare. So here goes, to give the goblin a fair start in a new one! A clear stage and no favour for the goblins, ladies and gentlemen, if you please.

The story of the goblins who stole a sexton

"In an old abbey town, down in this part of the country, a long, long while ago—so long that the story must be a true one, because our great-grandfathers implicitly believed it—there officiated as sexton and grave-digger in the churchyard, one Gabriel Grub. It by no means follows that because a man is a sexton and constantly surrounded by the emblems of mortality, therefore he should be a morose and melancholy man; your undertakers are the merriest fellows in the world; and I once had the honour of being on intimate terms with a mute, who in private life and off duty was as comical and jocose a little fellow as ever chirped out a devil-may-care song, without a hitch in his memory, or drained off the contents of a good stiff glass without stopping for breath. But notwithstanding these precedents to the contrary, Gabriel Grub was an ill-conditioned, cross-grained surly fellow—a morose and lonely man, who consorted with nobody but himself and an old wicker bottle, which fitted into his deep waistcoat pocket—and who eyed each merry face, as it passed him by, with such a deep scowl of malice and ill humour as it was difficult to meet without feeling something the worse for.

"A little before twilight, one Christmas Eve, Gabriel shouldered his spade, lighted his lantern, and betook himself towards the old churchyard; for he had got a grave to finish by next morning, and feeling very low, he thought it might raise his spirits, perhaps, if he went on with his work at once. As he went his way up the ancient street, he saw the cheerful light of the blazing fires gleam through the old casements and heard the loud laugh and the cheerful shouts of those who were assembled around them; he marked the bustling preparations for next day's cheer and smelt the numerous savoury odours consequent thereupon, as they steamed up from the kitchen-windows in clouds. All this was gall and wormwood to the heart of Gabriel Grub; and when groups of children bounded out of the houses, tripped across the road, and were met, before they could knock at the opposite door, by half a dozen curly-headed little rascals, who crowded round them as they flocked upstairs to spend the evening in their Christmas games, Gabriel smiled grimly and clutched the handle of his spade with a firmer grasp as he thought of measles, scarlet fever, thrush, hooping-cough, and a good many other sources of consolation besides.

"In this happy frame of mind, Gabriel strode along, returning a short, sullen growl to the good-humoured greetings of such of his neighbours as now and then passed him, until he turned into the dark lane which led to the churchyard. Now, Gabriel had been looking forward to reaching the dark lane because it was, generally speaking, a nice, gloomy, mournful place, into which the townspeople did not much care to go

except in broad daylight and when the sun was shining; consequently he was not a little indignant to hear
a young urchin roaring out some jolly song about a
merry Christmas, in this very sanctuary, which had
been called Coffin Lane ever since the days of the
old abbey and the time of the shaven-headed monks.
As Gabriel walked on and the voice drew nearer, he
found it proceeded from a small boy, who was hurrying along to join one of the little parties in the old street
and who, partly to keep himself company and partly
to prepare himself for the occasion, was shouting out
the song at the highest pitch of his lungs. So Gabriel
waited until the boy came up, and then dodged him
into a corner and rapped him over the head with his
lantern five or six times, to teach him to modulate his
voice. And as the boy hurried away with his hand to
his head, singing quite a different sort of tune, Gabriel
Grub chuckled very heartily to himself and entered the
churchyard, locking the gate behind him.

"He took off his coat, put down his lantern, and getting into the unfinished grave, worked at it for an hour
or so with right goodwill. But the earth was hardened
with the frost, and it was no very easy matter to break
it up and shovel it out; and although there was a moon,
it was a very young one, and shed little light upon the
grave, which was in the shadow of the church. At any
other time these obstacles would have made Gabriel
Grub very moody and miserable, but he was so well
pleased with having stopped the small boy's singing
that he took little heed of the scanty progress he had
made, and looked down into the grave, when he had
finished work for the night, with grim satisfaction,
murmuring as he gathered up his things:

"'Brave lodgings for one, brave lodgings for one,
A few feet of cold earth, when life is done;
A stone at the head, a stone at the feet,
A rich, juicy meal for the worms to eat;
Rank grass over head, and damp clay around,
Brave lodgings for one, these, in holy ground!

"'Ho! Ho!' laughed Gabriel Grub as he sat himself down on a flat tombstone which was a favourite resting-place of his, and drew forth his wicker bottle. 'A coffin at Christmas! A Christmas box. Ho! Ho! Ho!'

"'Ho! Ho! Ho!' repeated a voice which sounded close behind him.

"Gabriel paused, in some alarm, in the act of raising the wicker bottle to his lips, and looked round. The bottom of the oldest grave about him was not more still and quiet than the churchyard in the pale moonlight. The cold hoar-frost glistened on the tombstones and sparkled like rows of gems among the stone carvings of the old church. The snow lay hard and crisp upon the ground, and spread over the thickly strewn mounds of earth so white and smooth a cover that it seemed as if corpses lay there, hidden only by their winding-sheets. Not the faintest rustle broke the profound tranquility of the solemn scene. Sound itself appeared to be frozen up, all was so cold and still.

"'It was the echoes,' said Gabriel Grub, raising the bottle to his lips again.

"'It was *not*,' said a deep voice.

"Gabriel started up and stood rooted to the spot with astonishment and terror, for his eyes rested on a form that made his blood run cold.

"Seated on an upright tombstone close to him was a strange unearthly figure, whom Gabriel felt at once was no being of this world. His long fantastic legs, which might have reached the ground, were cocked up and crossed after a quaint, fantastic fashion; his sinewy arms were bare; and his hands rested on his knees. On his short round body he wore a close covering, ornamented with small slashes; a short cloak dangled at his back; the collar was cut into curious peaks, which served the goblin in lieu of ruff or neckerchief; and his shoes curled up at his toes into long points. On his head he wore a broad-brimmed sugar-loaf hat, garnished with a single feather. The hat was covered with the white frost; and the goblin looked as if he had sat on the same tombstone very comfortably for two or three hundred years. He was sitting perfectly still; his tongue was put out, as if in derision; and he was grinning at Gabriel Grub with such a grin as only a goblin could call up.

" 'It was *not* the echoes,' said the goblin.

"Gabriel Grub was paralysed and could make no reply.

" 'What do you do here on Christmas Eve?' said the goblin sternly.

" 'I came to dig a grave, sir,' stammered Gabriel Grub.

" 'What man wanders among graves and church-yards on such a night as this?' cried the goblin.

" 'Gabriel Grub! Gabriel Grub!' screamed a wild chorus of voices that seemed to fill the churchyard. Gabriel looked fearfully round—nothing was to be seen.

" 'What have you got in that bottle?' said the goblin.

" 'Hollands, sir,' replied the sexton, trembling more than ever; for he had bought it of the smugglers, and he thought that perhaps his questioner might be in the excise department of the goblins.

" 'Who drinks Hollands alone, and in a churchyard, on such a night as this?' said the goblin.

" 'Gabriel Grub! Gabriel Grub!' exclaimed the wild voices again.

"The goblin leered maliciously at the terrified sexton and then, raising his voice, exclaimed: 'And who, then, is our fair and lawful prize?'

"To this inquiry the invisible chorus replied, in a strain that sounded like the voices of many choristers singing to the mighty swell of the old church-organ—a strain that seemed borne to the sexton's ears upon a wild wind, and to die away as it passed onward; but the burden of the reply was still the same—'Gabriel Grub! Gabriel Grub!'

"The goblin grinned a broader grin than before as he said, 'Well, Gabriel, what do you say to this?'

"The sexton gasped for breath.

" 'What do you think of this, Gabriel?' said the goblin, kicking up his feet in the air on either side of the tombstone, and looking at the turned-up points with as much complacency as if he had been contemplating the most fashionable pair of Wellingtons in all Bond Street.

" 'It's—it's—very curious, sir,' replied the sexton, half dead with fright; 'very curious, and very pretty, but I think I'll go back and finish my work, sir, if you please.'

" 'Work!' said the goblin. 'What work?'

" 'The grave, sir; making the grave,' stammered the sexton.

" 'Oh, the grave, eh?' said the goblin. 'Who makes

graves at a time when all other men are merry and takes a pleasure in it?'

"Again the mysterious voices replied, 'Gabriel Grub! Gabriel Grub!'

"'I'm afraid my friends want you, Gabriel,' said the goblin, thrusting his tongue further into his cheek than ever—and a most astonishing tongue it was—'I'm afraid my friends want you, Gabriel,' said the goblin.

"'Under favour, sir,' replied the horror-stricken sexton, 'I don't think they can, sir; they don't know me, sir; I don't think the gentlemen have ever seen me, sir.'

"'Oh, yes, they have,' replied the goblin; 'we know the man with the sulky face and grim scowl that came down the street to-night, throwing his evil looks at the children and grasping his burying spade tighter. We know the man who struck the boy in the envious malice of his heart because the boy could be merry and he could not. We know him, we know him.'

"Here the goblin gave a loud shrill laugh, which the echoes returned twentyfold, and throwing his legs up in the air, stood upon his head or, rather, upon the very point of his sugar-loaf hat, on the narrow edge of the tombstone; whence he threw a somerset with extraordinary agility, right to the sexton's feet, at which he planted himself in the attitude in which tailors generally sit upon the shop-board.

"'I—I—am afraid I must leave you, sir,' said the sexton, making an effort to move.

"'Leave us!' said the goblin. 'Gabriel Grub is going to leave us. Ho! Ho! Ho!'

"As the goblin laughed, the sexton observed for one instant a brilliant illumination within the windows of the church, as if the whole building were lighted up;

it disappeared, the organ pealed forth a lively air, and whole troops of goblins, the very counterpart of the first one, poured into the churchyard and began playing at leap-frog with the tombstones, never stopping for an instant to take a breath, but 'overing' the highest among them, one after the other, with the utmost marvellous dexterity. The first goblin was a most astonishing leaper, and none of the others could come near him; even in the extremity of his terror, the sexton could not help observing that while his friends were content to leap over the common-sized gravestones, the first one took the family vaults, iron railings and all, with as much ease as if they had been so many street-posts.

"At last the game reached to a most exciting pitch; the organ played quicker and quicker; and the goblins leaped faster and faster—coiling themselves up, rolling head over heels upon the ground, and bounding over the tombstones like footballs. The sexton's brain whirled round with the rapidity of the motion he beheld, and his legs reeled beneath him as the spirits flew before his eyes, when the goblin king, suddenly darting towards him, laid his hand upon his collar and sank with him through the earth.

"When Gabriel Grub had had time to fetch his breath, which the rapidity of his descent had for the moment taken away, he found himself in what appeared to be a large cavern, surrounded on all sides by crowds of goblins, ugly and grim; in the centre of the room, on an elevated seat, was stationed his friend of the churchyard; and close beside him stood Gabriel Grub himself, without power of motion.

"'Cold to-night,' said the king of the goblins, 'very cold. A glass of something warm here!'

"At this command, half a dozen officious goblins,

with a perpetual smile upon their faces, whom Gabriel Grub imagined to be courtiers on that account, hastily disappeared, and presently returned with a goblet of liquid fire, which they presented to the king.

"'Ah!' cried the goblin, whose cheeks and throat were transparent as he tossed down the flame. 'This warms one, indeed! Bring a bumper of the same for Mr. Grub.'

"It was in vain for the unfortunate sexton to protest that he was not in the habit of taking anything warm at night; one of the goblins held him while another poured the blazing liquid down his throat; the whole assembly screeched with laughter as he coughed and choked and wiped away the tears which gushed plentifully from his eyes after swallowing the burning draught.

"'And now,' said the king, fantastically poking the taper corner of his sugar-loaf hat into the sexton's eye, and thereby occasioning him the most exquisite pain, 'and now, show the man of misery and gloom a few of the pictures from our own great storehouse!'

"As the goblin said this, a thick cloud which obscured the remoter end of the cavern rolled gradually away and disclosed, apparently at a great distance, a small and scantily furnished, but neat and clean, apartment. A crowd of little children were gathered round a bright fire, clinging to their mother's gown and gamboling around her chair. The mother occasionally rose and drew aside the window-curtain, as if to look for some expected object; a frugal meal was spread upon the table; and an elbow chair was placed near the fire. A knock was heard at the door; the mother opened it, and the children crowded round her and clapped their hands for joy as their father entered. He was wet and weary, and shook the snow from his garments as the children crowded round him, and seizing his cloak, hat, stick, and gloves, with busy zeal, ran with them from the room. Then, as he sat down to his meal before the fire, the children climbed about his knee, and the mother sat by his side, and all seemed happiness and comfort.

"But a change came upon the view, almost imperceptibly. The scene was altered to a small bedroom, where the fairest and youngest child lay dying; the roses had fled from his cheek, and the light from his eye; and even as the sexton looked upon him, with an interest he had never felt or known before, he died. His young brothers and sisters crowded round his little bed and seized his tiny hand, so cold and heavy; but they shrunk back from its touch and looked with awe on his infant face; for calm and tranquil as it was, and sleeping in rest and peace as the beautiful child seemed to be, they saw that he was dead, and they knew that he was an angel looking down upon and blessing them from a bright and happy Heaven.

"Again the light cloud passed across the picture, and again the subject changed. The father and mother were old and helpless now, and the number of those about them was diminished more than half; but content and cheerfulness sat on every face and beamed in every eye as they crowded round the fireside, and told and listened to old stories of earlier and bygone days. Slowly and peacefully, the father sank into the grave, and soon after, the sharer of all his cares and troubles followed him to a place of rest. The few who yet survived them knelt by their tomb and watered the green turf which covered it with their tears, then rose and turned away, sadly and mournfully, but not with bitter cries or despairing lamentations, for they knew that they should one day meet again; and once more they mixed with the busy world, and their content and cheerfulness were restored. The cloud settled upon the picture and concealed it from the sexton's view.

" 'What do you think of *that*?' said the goblin, turning his large face towards Gabriel Grub.

"Gabriel murmured out something about its being very pretty, and looked somewhat ashamed as the goblin bent his fiery eyes upon him.

" '*You* a miserable man!' said the goblin in a tone of excessive contempt. 'You!' He appeared disposed to add more, but indignation choked his utterance, so he lifted up one of his very pliable legs and, flourishing it above his head a little to ensure his aim, administered a good sound kick to Gabriel Grub; immediately after which, all the goblins-in-waiting crowded round the wretched sexton and kicked him without mercy, according to the established and invariable custom of courtiers upon earth, who kick whom royalty kicks and hug whom royalty hugs.

" 'Show him some more!' said the king of the goblins.

"At these words the cloud was dispelled and a rich and beautiful landscape was disclosed to view—there is just such another, to this day, within half a mile of the old abbey town. The sun shone from out the clear blue sky, the water sparkled beneath his rays, and the trees looked greener and the flowers more gay beneath his cheering influence. The water rippled on with a pleasant sound; the trees rustled in the light wind that murmured among their leaves; the birds sang upon the boughs; and the lark carolled on high her welcome to the morning. Yes, it was morning—the bright, balmy morning of summer; the minutest leaf, the smallest blade of grass, was instinct with life. The ant crept forth to her daily toil, the butterfly fluttered and basked in the warm rays of the sun; myriads of insects spread their transparent wings and revelled in their brief but happy existence. Man walked forth, elated with the scene; and all was brightness and splendour.

"'You a miserable man!' said the king of the goblins in a more contemptuous tone than before. And again the king of the goblins gave his leg a flourish; again it descended on the shoulders of the sexton; and again the attendant goblins imitated the example of their chief.

"Many a time the cloud went and came, and many a lesson it taught to Gabriel Grub, who, although his shoulders smarted with pain from the frequent applications of the goblins' feet, looked on with an interest that nothing could diminish. He saw that men who worked hard and earned their scanty bread with lives of labour were cheerful and happy; and that to the most ignorant, the sweet face of nature was a never-failing source of cheerfulness and joy. He saw those who had been delicately nurtured and tenderly brought up, cheerful under privations and superior to suffering that would have crushed many of a rougher grain, because they bore within their own bosoms the material of happiness, contentment, and peace. He saw that women, the tenderest and most fragile of all God's creatures, were the oftenest superior to sorrow, adversity, and distress; and he saw that it was because they bore in their own hearts an inexhaustible wellspring of affection and devotion. Above all, he saw that men like himself, who snarled at the mirth and cheerfulness of others, were the foulest weeds on the fair surface of the earth; and setting all the good of the world against the evil, he came to the conclusion that it was a very decent and respectable sort of world after all. No sooner had he formed it than the cloud which closed over the last picture seemed to settle on his senses and lull him to repose. One by one, the goblins faded from his sight; and as the last one disappeared he sunk to sleep.

"The day had broken when Gabriel Grub awoke and found himself lying, at full length, on the flat gravestone in the churchyard, with the wicker bottle lying empty by his side, and his coat, spade, and lantern, all well whitened by the last night's frost, scattered on the ground. The stone on which he had first seen the goblin seated stood bolt upright before him, and the grave at which he had worked the night before was not far off. At first he began to doubt the reality of his adventures, but the acute pain in his shoulders when he attempted to rise assured him that the kicking of the goblins was certainly not ideal. He was staggered again by observing no traces of footsteps in the snow, on which the goblins had played at leap-frog with the gravestones, but he speedily accounted for this circumstance when he remembered that, being spirits, they would leave no visible impression behind them. So, Gabriel Grub got on his feet as well as he could, for the pain in his back, and brushing the frost off his coat, put it on and turned his face towards the town.

"But he was an altered man, and he could not bear the thought of returning to a place where his repentance would be scoffed at and his reformation disbelieved. He hesitated for a few moments, and then turned away to wander where he might and seek his bread elsewhere.

"The lantern, the spade, and the wicker bottle were found that day in the churchyard. There were a great many speculations about the sexton's fate at first, but it was speedily determined that he had been carried away by the goblins; and there were not wanting some very credible witnesses who had distinctly seen him whisked through the air on the back of a chestnut horse blind of one eye, with the hind-quarters of a lion and the tail of a bear. At length all this was devoutly believed; and the new sexton used to exhibit to the curious, for a trifling emolument, a good-sized piece of the church-weathercock, which had been accidentally kicked off by the aforesaid horse in his aerial flight, and picked up by himself in the churchyard a year or two afterwards.

"Unfortunately, these stories were somewhat disturbed by the unlooked-for reappearance of Gabriel Grub himself, some ten years afterwards, a ragged, contented, rheumatic old man. He told his story to the clergyman and also to the mayor; and in course of time it began to be received as a matter of history, in which form it has continued down to this very day. The believers in the weathercock tale, having misplaced their confidence once, were not easily prevailed upon to part with it again, so they looked as wise as they could, shrugged their shoulders, touched their foreheads, and murmured something about Gabriel Grub having drunk all the Hollands and then fallen asleep on the flat tombstone; and they affected to explain what he supposed he had witnessed in the goblins' cavern by saying that he had seen the world and grown wiser. But this opinion, which was by no means a popular one at any time, gradually died off; and be the matter how it may, as Gabriel Grub was afflicted with rheumatism to the end of his days, this story has at least one moral if it teach no better one—and that is that if a man turn sulky and drink by himself at Christmas-time, he may make up his mind to be not a bit the better for it; let the spirits be never so good, or let them be even as many degrees beyond proof as those which Gabriel saw in the goblin's cavern."

Afterword

In one way or another, I have lived with my great-great-grandfather's *A Christmas Carol* for my entire life. One of my earliest Christmas memories was sitting, on Christmas Eve, as the *Carol* was read aloud to all the children in the house before bed. I sat transfixed, listening attentively, and was astonished when it was revealed that Scrooge hadn't "missed it!" (page 99) and could, in fact, enjoy his Christmas day with the rest of us. How could that be? He had been traveling with the spirits for three days; Charles Dickens had told us so. Scrooge had gone to bed and slept through each night, prior to being awoken by the next spectral figure. The answer, of course, lay with my great-great-grandfather's skill as a conjuror. With sleight of hand—or of word, in this case—he had led us to believe one thing, before revealing the opposite. And I, for one, was astounded.

As years went on, I never tired of listening and began to look forward to particular phrases that brought a simple story to wonderful, vivid life:

But how much greater was his horror when, the phantom taking off the bandage round his head, as if it were too warm to wear indoors, his lower jaw dropped down upon his breast! (page 20)

In came Mrs. Fezziwig, one vast, substantial smile. (page 39)

Built upon a dismal reef of sunken rocks, some leagues or so from shore, on which the waters chafed and dashed, the wild year through, there stood a solitary lighthouse. (page 67)

and so many others.

Years have passed and now, as an actor, I am fortunate to perform *A Christmas Carol* as a one-man show and see how the story still amazes and delights. I have lost count of the amount of times that I have strode onto the stage and delivered one of the most memorable opening lines in literature: "Marley was dead, to begin with" (page 3), but I have never grown tired or bored of it. Quite the opposite in fact, it still sends a frisson of excitement through me as I anticipate the adventure to come.

Why is *A Christmas Carol* so popular and why has it lasted well into its second century? I think, like any good story, it works on many different levels and has something for all. At its core, it is a wonderfully positive story about redemption that tells us however dark a person may be, there is always the chance to come out the other side and live a better life. We all need that affirmation, and to be given it every year is a cleansing process for all.

But the cleansing could never work if Ebenezer

Scrooge were only a puppet, a caricature. We have to see something of ourselves within him, and we need to see enough to make us stop and think, "There but for the grace of God, go I."

A Christmas Carol wasn't an original idea. Charles Dickens had tried it out some seven years previously in his first novel, *The Pickwick Papers*. One of the characters begins to regale his guests with the "Story of the Goblins Who Stole a Sexton," which features a grave-digger by the name of Gabriel Grub,

> ... an ill-conditioned, cross-grained surly fellow—a morose and lonely man, who consorted with nobody but himself and an old wicker bottle, which fitted into his deep waistcoat pocket—and who eyed each merry face, as it passed him by, with such a deep scowl of malice and ill humour as it was difficult to meet without feeling something the worse for.   (pages 167–68)

Compare that to the first description of Ebenezer Scrooge in the *Carol*:

> Oh! But he was a tight-fisted hand at the grindstone, Scrooge! a squeezing, wrenching, grasping, scraping, clutching, covetous, old sinner! Hard and sharp as flint, from which no steel had ever struck out generous fire, secret, and self-contained, and solitary as an oyster. The cold within him froze his old features, nipped his pointed nose, shriveled his cheek, stiffened his gait, made his eyes red, his thin lips blue. . . .   (page 4)

Gabriel Grub's description starts with repulsive physical details and alerts us that he is certainly one to steer clear of. Scrooge's description, although equally unpleasant, is businesslike. We may not like the sound of him, but there is no doubt that he cares about his job, which under other circumstances would be seen as an attribute.

The stories continue. Gabriel Grub's passion for his work sees him digging the frozen earth on Christmas Eve. Ebenezer Scrooge is a successful businessman in the thriving heart of the City of London.

Gabriel reacts to a young boy singing a Christmas song by rapping

> him over the head with his lantern five or six times, to teach him to modulate his voice. And as the boy hurried away with his hand to his head, singing quite a different sort of tune, Gabriel Grub chuckled very heartily to himself and entered the churchyard, locking the gate behind him. (page 169)

Ebenezer reacts to the same disruption by seizing a "ruler with such energy of action, that the singer fled in terror, leaving the keyhole to the fog and even more congenial frost" (page 12).

Again, there are similarities, but Scrooge's response, though violent, does no physical harm. In contrast, beating a boy round the head with a lantern is certainly the work of a vicious man.

Charles Dickens has been very careful to make Scrooge a character that we don't like, but can almost admire for his single-mindedness. To cement the point he brings two charity collectors into the counting-house. At first we are horrified that Scrooge is so terse and short with them, sending them away with nothing, but actually, his arguments are quite valid. In short, he states that he works hard to make a living, he is not a crook, and he pays his taxes. Is it his fault if the poor are not properly provided for by the government?

Once more, Dickens challenges the readers to look into themselves. This is a well-made business argument, and let's face it, how many times have you brushed passed a charity collection in a shopping mall on Christmas Eve?

It is often said that only fear of the Ghost of Christmas Yet to Come and the vision of his own death break through to Scrooge, but that is not true. Dickens brilliantly places little moments throughout all of Scrooge's travels that chip away at his stony exterior. The first of these takes us back to the carol-singing boy who has been scared away by the threat of a ruler.

The Ghost of Christmas Past has taken Scrooge back to see his childhood, and for a moment he is laughing with his friends, recognizing the road, the town, the church, and the school. It is in the school that Ebenezer first sees himself, lonely, abandoned, and neglected at Christmas. What is his first response? He says " 'Poor boy' " (page 35), which we may take to be a self-pitying thought, but he follows it up by saying, " 'I wish' " (page 35). When prompted by the Ghost, he admits that he wished he'd given the caroler at his door " 'something' " (page 35). Already he is changing.

Because *A Christmas Carol* is a full story, whereas "Gabriel Grub" is just an episode, we are allowed to discover much more about Ebenezer's background, and at every turn we become ever more sympathetic to him.

In addition to being abandoned at school, there is a hint that Scrooge may have had to face a violent father at home. Scrooge's sister, Fan, at last comes to the school to tell him he is to be taken home, explaining:

> "Father is so much kinder than he used to be, that home's like Heaven! He spoke so gently to me one dear night when I was going to bed that I was not afraid to ask him once more if you might come home; and he said Yes, you should." (page 36)

But, even though this should have been a celebratory moment in young Scrooge's life, the language used by Dickens is that of fear:

> A terrible voice in the hall cried, "Bring down Master Scrooge's box, there!" and in the hall appeared the schoolmaster himself, who glared on Master Scrooge with a ferocious condescension, and threw him into a dreadful state of mind by shaking hands with him. (page 36)

The next scene comes suddenly and brings Scrooge straight into business (no loving reunion with his father). Here, at Mr. Fezziwig's, Scrooge is at his happiest! He watches in delight as the Christmas party unfolds before him, and now the language is exhausting in its joyfulness:

> "Hilli-Ho!" cried old Fezziwig, skipping down from the high desk with wonderful agility. "Clear away, my lads, and let's have lots of room here! Hilli-Ho. Dick! Chirrup, Ebenezer!" (page 38)

As the scene ends Scrooge is suddenly brought face-to-face with another realization: all that happiness, all that energy, all those celebrations, all those memories were made possible by one man: his employer. Again he thinks back to the previous evening, when he had only grudgingly agreed to let Bob Cratchit have one day off at Christmas. The responsibility of the employer is brought back to Ebenezer again with the Ghost of Christmas Present.

All throughout the travels with the Ghost of Christmas Past, we are allowed to sympathize with Ebenezer. When the Ghost of Christmas Present appears, the tone is different. Instead of being voyeurs, we are now traveling *with* Scrooge and sharing the effects of his actions. The trip to the Cratchits' house shows us the gulf between Mr. Fezziwig and Scrooge when it comes to staff relations. But even there, despite Mrs. Cratchit's grumbling, Bob Cratchit encourages the family to raise a glass in honor of " 'Mr. Scrooge, the Founder of the Feast' " (page 63).

At this point, Dickens suddenly turns us on our heads. Somehow, as readers, we have accepted that we are traveling with ghosts, each with his own domain (past, present and future), and that we will be allowed to observe but not interfere in the scenes. Suddenly, however, that changes and the Ghost of Christmas Present starts predicting the future!

Scrooge asks if Tiny Tim will live and the Ghost of Christmas *Present* tells him that if he doesn't change his ways, the boy will die, and the chair and crutch will be carefully preserved. As fast as we have come to terms with that, we are back to the present and the Cratchits' celebrations again.

Some reviews see this as a weakness in the structure of the book, but to me this is the moment when we realize that Charles Dickens is playing with time. This is the moment that makes it possible for the spirits to "'have done it all in one night'" (page 99). This is the sleight of hand of the master conjuror.

The vision of the present carries on, the Cratchits finish their Christmas lunch, and just as we feel that we are accepted into the family celebrations: *Whoosh!* We are away again, and now Dickens hurls us around the globe, to a "bleak and desert moor, where monstrous masses of rude stone were cast about, as though it were a burial-place of giants" (page 66). We pass through a wall of mud and stone, but we do not linger. Suddenly we are off again to a ship being tossed on the black and heaving sea, and then *bang!* we are back in the comfortable surroundings of Scrooge's nephew's house.

At last, we have returned to a world of normality, a Christmas party, observing happiness and good cheer. This time Scrooge doesn't remain distant, morose, or reflective but actually joins in with the games and pleads with the Ghost to allow him to stay for an extra half hour.

We now feel that the lesson has been learned and that Ebenezer Scrooge finally understands Christmas, but there is another sting in the tail. Scrooge suddenly notices that the spirit is growing old, and when he asks about it is told, "'My life on this globe is very brief. . . . It ends tonight. . . . Tonight at midnight'" (page 75). We are once again back to a conventional day.

The time is eleven forty-five, and the Ghost of Christmas Present leaves us with the terrifying vision of the two skeletal children, Ignorance and Want. This is one of the most powerful images of the book and one that is meant for us, the readers, whether in 1843 or 2008. Scrooge is well on the way to realization, but we still need work!

The final scenes with the Ghost of Christmas Yet to

Come (Why not Future? I wonder) are dark and Gothic in their intensity. There is a nightmare quality about them, especially as the spirit seems to have no face and never speaks. It can be no coincidence that when J. K. Rowling decided on the form of the Dementors in the Harry Potter series, she used this exact image.

The language changes again and becomes almost repulsive:

> They left the busy scene, and went into an obscure part of the town, where Scrooge had never penetrated before, although he recognized its situation, and its bad repute. The ways were foul and narrow, the shops and the houses wretched, the people half naked, drunken, slipshod, ugly. Alleys and archways, like so many cesspools, disgorged their offenses of smell, and dirt, and life, upon the straggling streets; and the whole quarter reeked with crime, with filth and misery.   (page 81)

From now on Scrooge is battered by images of the effect of his own death: to some it is just a minor topic of conversation to pass the time; to others it is an opportunity for a small profit; and to a struggling family in debt to Scrooge, it is a time of celebration. Each vision batters Scrooge ever more until suddenly he sees real emotion regarding a death. The Ghost of Christmas Present's prophecy has come true, and Tiny Tim is dead. Bob Cratchit is broken, and there is nothing to be done. It is too late.

As the Ghost takes Ebenezer Scrooge to his own grave, an idea suddenly hits him: there *is* a chance! The Ghost of Christmas Present said, "'If these shadows remain unaltered . . .'" (page 62). As Scrooge comes to this realization, he is back in his bedroom on Christmas morning. He hasn't missed it! The Spirits have done it all in one night! And that is where we came in.

It really is a story that takes you on a journey and mangles you up along the way, before releasing you at its end, a better person.

We all have some Ebenezer Scrooge in us, but that is fine. There is always hope. We all have some of the struggling Bob Cratchit in us, and that is fine too. There is always hope. *A Christmas Carol* is a story of hope for all of us.

I started by describing my childhood memories of listening to the *Carol* being read to us. Let me close with my father's memories of the same event. He listened to his grandfather reading the story, but was a bit young to really appreciate it. However one thing stuck in his memory: at the point of the story when Scrooge jumps up on Christmas morning and shouts " 'Hallo! Whoop! Hallo here!' " (page 98), my father recalled that his grandfather's false teeth flew out! What makes the story even more amazing is that the grandfather in question was Sir Henry Fielding Dickens KC, who had stood in the Saint James' Hall in London and watched *his* father, Charles Dickens, perform his "ghostly little book."

We in the Dickens family have a wonderful legacy that we are so proud of, and it has been a delight to share with you my thoughts on *A Christmas Carol*.

Happy Christmas . . . all the year!

—Gerald Charles Dickens
July 2008

Selected
Bibliography

WORKS BY CHARLES DICKENS

Sketches by Boz, 1836, 1839 Sketches and Stories
The Posthumous Papers of the Pickwick Club, 1837 Novel
Oliver Twist; or, the Parish Boy's Progress, 1838 Novel
The Life and Adventures of Nicholas Nickleby, 1839 Novel
The Old Curiosity Shop, 1841 Novel
Barnaby Rudge, 1841 Novel
American Notes: For General Circulation, 1842 Travel Book
A Christmas Carol: in Prose, 1843 Christmas Book
The Life and Adventures of Martin Chuzzlewit, 1844 Novel
The Chimes, 1844 Christmas Book
The Cricket on the Hearth, 1845 Christmas Book
Pictures from Italy, 1846 Travel Book
The Battle of Life: A Love Story, 1846 Christmas Book
Dealings with the Firm of Dombey and Son, 1848 Novel
The Haunted Man and the Ghost's Bargain, 1848 Christmas Book
The Personal History of David Copperfield, 1850 Novel
A Child's History of England, 1852, 1853, 1854 History
Bleak House, 1853 Novel

Hard Times: For These Times, 1854 Novel

Little Dorrit, 1857 Novel

The Lazy Tour of Two Idle Apprentices (with Wilkie Collins), 1857 Travel Book

Reprinted Pieces, 1858 Collection of Magazine Articles

A Tale of Two Cities, 1859 Novel

Great Expectations, 1861 Novel

The Uncommercial Traveler, 1861, 1868 Collection of Magazine Articles

Our Mutual Friend, 1865 Novel

"George Silverman's Explanation," 1868 Story

The Mystery of Edwin Drood (unfinished), 1870 Novel

SELECTED BIOGRAPHY AND CRITICISM

Ackroyd, Peter. *Dickens.* New York and London: Harper-Collins, 1990.

Andrews, Malcolm. *Dickens and the Grown-up Child.* London: Macmillan, 1994.

Atwood, Margaret. *Payback: Debt and the Shadow Side of Wealth.* Toronto: Anansi, 2008.

Born, Daniel. *The Birth of Liberal Guilt in the English Novel.* Chapel Hill: University of North Caroline Press, 1995.

Butt, John, and Kathleen Tillotson. *Dickens at Work.* Fairlawn, NJ: Essential Books, 1958.

Chesterton, G. K. *Appreciations and Criticism of the Works of Charles Dickens.* New York: Dutton, 1911.

———. *Charles Dickens: The Last of the Great Men.* Foreword by Alexander Woolcott. New York: The Press of the Reader's Club, 1942.

Collins, Philip. *Dickens and Crime.* 3d ed. London: St. Martin's Press, 1994.

Epstein, Norrie, ed. *The Friendly Dickens.* New York: Penguin, 2001.

Foor, Sheila M. *Dickens's Rhetoric*. New York: Lang, 1993.

Forster, John. *The Life of Charles Dickens*. London: Dutton, 1966.

Glavin, John. *Dickens on Screen*. Cambridge: Cambridge University Press, 2003.

Gillooly, Eileen, and Deirdre David, eds. *Contemporary Dickens*. Columbus: The Ohio State University Press, 2009.

Guida, Fred. *A Christmas Carol and Its Adaptations: A Critical Examination of Dickens's Story and Its Productions on Screen and Television*. Jefferson, NC: McFarland & Company, Inc., 2006.

House, Humphrey. *The Dickens World*. London and New York: Oxford University Press, 1941.

Johnson, Edgar. *Charles Dickens: His Tragedy and Triumph*. 2 vols. New York: Simon & Schuster, 1952.

Kaplan, Fred. *Dickens: A Biography*. New York: William Morrow and Co., 1988.

Leavis, F. R., and Q. D. Leavis. *Dickens the Novelist*. New York: Pantheon, 1971.

McAleavey, Maia. "Soul-Mates: *David Copperfield*'s Angelic Bigamy" in *Victorian Studies*, Vol. 52, No. 2 (Winter 2010), pp.191–218.

Miller, J. Hillis. *Charles Dickens: The World of His Novels*. Cambridge, MA: Harvard University Press, 1958.

Orwell, George. "Charles Dickens." In *The Collected Essays, Journalism and Letters of George Orwell*. Vol. I. Ed. Sonia Orwell and Ian Angus. Harmondsworth, England: Penguin, 1972.

Parker, David. *Christmas and Charles Dickens*. New York: AMS Press, Inc., 2005.

Schlicke, Paul, ed. *Oxford Reader's Companion to Dickens*. Oxford: Oxford University Press, 1999.

Slater, Michael. *Charles Dickens*. New Haven, CT: Yale University Press, 2009.

Smiley, Jane. *Charles Dickens*. Penguin Lives. New York: Lipper/Viking, 2001.

Stone, Harry. *Dickens and the Invisible World: Fairy Tales, Fantasy, and Novel-Making*. Bloomington: Indiana University Press, 1979.

Tomalin, Claire. *The Invisible Woman: The Story of Nelly Ternan and Charles Dickens*. New York: Alfred A. Knopf, 1991.

Welsh, Alexander. *The City of Dickens*. Cambridge, MA: Harvard University Press, 1986.

Wilson, Edmund. "Dickens: The Two Scrooges." In his *The Wound and the Bow*. New York: Oxford University Press, 1947.